This
latest
perio
- Ph
- Visi

Di

Three-times Golden Heart® finalist **Tina Beckett** learned to pack her suitcases almost before she learned to read. Born to a military family, she has lived in the United States, Puerto Rico, Portugal and Brazil. In addition to travelling, Tina loves to cuddle with her pug, Alex, spend time with her family, and hit the trails on her horse. Learn more about Tina from her website, or 'friend' her on Facebook.

THE SURGEON'S SURPRISE BABY

TINA BECKETT

MILLS & BOON

First published in Great Britain 2019
by Mills & Boon, an imprint of HarperCollins*Publishers*
1 London Bridge Street, London, SE1 9GF

Large Print edition 2019

© 2019 Tina Beckett

ISBN: 978-0-263-07861-9

MIX
Paper from
responsible sources
FSC® C007454

This book is produced from independently certified FSC™ paper to ensure responsible forest management. For more information visit www.harpercollins.co.uk/green.

Printed and bound in Great Britain
by CPI Group (UK) Ltd, Croydon, CR0 4YY

To my husband:
thank you for my chickens!

PROLOGUE

"WELL, I'M NO longer your boss."

Luca Venezio stared at her as if she'd lost her mind. No longer his boss? Was that all she had to say to him? The obvious relief in her voice told him that she'd been anxious to wield that particular ax. Only she'd just done it in a room full of his colleagues, who had suffered a similar fate. He'd stayed behind after the others had all filed out dejectedly.

She was perched on her desk, looking just as gorgeous as she had a year ago, when he'd first stepped into her neurology department. It had taken him a while, but he'd finally convinced her to look past her reservations about engaging in a workplace relationship and see what they could be like together.

And it had been good. So very good.

He took a step closer. "Is that all you have to say to me, Elyse?"

Her head tilted as if she truly couldn't understand what the problem was. Was this an American thing that he hadn't yet grasped? Just when he thought he was understanding this culture, the woman in front of him threw something into the mix that had him reeling.

Italy was suddenly beckoning him home. But he wasn't leaving without a fight.

She slid from her desk and stood in front of him. "Don't you see? This could be a good thing."

No. He didn't see it. No matter how he looked at it.

She drove him insane. With want. With need. And now was no different.

"Do you want me gone, is that it?"

She took his hands in hers, before her hands slid up his forearms. "Are we talking about from the hospital? Or from my life?"

It was one and the same to Luca. It felt like they'd been trapped in a game of tug-of-war ever since their first date. The harder he pulled her toward him, the more she seemed to resist letting him get close to her, and he didn't understand why. They were in a relationship, only nothing was easy. Except the sex.

And that had been mind-blowing. Maybe part of that was the uncertainty of it all. Maybe it had lent an air of desperation to their lovemaking.

Her green eyes stared into his, and the crazy thing was, he could swear he saw a hint of lust in there, even though she'd just fired him. Had she gotten off on delivering that death blow to all those people?

No. That wasn't the Elyse he'd known these past few months.

"What is it you want from me, Elyse?"

"Don't you know?"

He didn't. Not at all, but he was tired of playing guessing games with her. He cupped her face, trying to make sense of it all, but the swirling in his head gave him no time to think. No time to ask any questions. Instead, the refuge they'd sought after each fight opened its door and whispered in his ear, promising it would all be okay.

He no longer believed it. But his blood was stirring in his veins, sending waves of heat through him. Even as her lips tilted up, telling him what she wanted, he was already there, the kiss scorching hot, just as it always was.

His tongue met hers, his hands going under her ass and sitting her back on her desk. The sound of her shoes hitting the floor one at a time and her hands going to his waist and tugging him forward between her legs answered his earlier question about what she wanted.

Hell. There was no question as to that. *Grazie a Dio* he'd locked the door behind him, thinking that what he'd had to say to her he wanted said in private. Right now, though, the last thing he wanted to do was talk.

And he was so hot. So ready. Just as he always was for her.

The desk was wide, the middle bare of anything.

Made for sex.

He grabbed hold of her wrists and tugged her hands away so that he could take a step back to unzip.

The sight of Elyse licking her lips was his undoing.

He came back to her, reaching under her skirt to yank her boy shorts down, tossing them away. Then he eased her down until her back was flat against her desk, her breasts jutting upward, the outline of her nipples plainly visible beneath the thin white blouse.

"Do you want me?" His hands palmed the smooth skin of her hips and tugged her to the very edge of the desk.

She bit her lip, her legs twining around his until he was pressed tight against her, his hard flesh finding a wet heat that destroyed any hopes of prolonging this. He drove home, her sharp cry ending on a moan, her hips moving as if to seat him even deeper.

"*Dio*, Elyse…" His eyes closed, trying to grasp at any shred of control and finding nothing there.

His thumb moved from her hip to her center, hoping to help things along, but the second he touched her, she exploded around him, her gasped "Yes," sending him over the edge. Bracing his hands on the desk, he plunged home again and again, his body spasming so hard his vision went white for a brief instant. Still he thrust, unwilling for the moment to end.

Because that's exactly what it would do. What it needed to do.

His movements slowed, reality slowly filtering back in.

Hell. As good as this was, it had solved nothing.

Nothing.

The job had been the thing that had held him there, made him keep trying, even as she burned hot and then cold.

But now she'd killed the job. And in doing that, the relationship. What they said about goodbye sex was evidently true.

He didn't try to kiss her, just moved away, zipping himself back in, even as she sat up on the desk.

"What's wrong?"

Was she really asking him that? Everything was wrong. But he was about to make it right.

"Did you put my name on that list of people to be fired?"

She frowned, coming off the desk, retrieving her undergarment, turning away from him as she slid them over her legs. She didn't answer as, with her back still turned, she pushed her feet into her shoes, black high-heeled pumps that he had always found so sexy.

By the time she finally turned around, his

last shred of patience had disappeared and he no longer needed a response. "You know what? It doesn't matter. You've been pushing me away ever since I got here, so I'm finally giving you your wish. I'm leaving. Going back to Italy. You actually did me a favor in firing me, so thank you."

He put a hand on the doorknob, half thinking she would call his name and tell him it was all a big mistake. Tell him that she didn't want him to go. He tensed, knowing that even if she did he was no longer willing to go on as they had been. Maybe he'd revisit that decision in a week…in a month. But right now, he needed time to think things through.

Except there was no sound from behind him as he opened the door. As he stepped through it. As he closed it.

Maybe that was all the thinking he needed to do.

So he started walking. And kept on walking until he was away from the hospital and on his way out of her life.

CHAPTER ONE

"I'M FINALLY GIVING you your wish."

Elyse Tenner hesitated, those words ringing in her ears just as fresh and sharp today as they'd done a little over a year ago.

Luca leaving hadn't been what she'd wanted. But it had evidently been what he'd wanted.

The entry door to the upscale clinic—complete with ornate scrollwork carved into the stone around it—was right in front of her. But she couldn't make herself open it.

Not yet.

It had been easier to find him than she'd thought. And yet it was the hardest thing she'd ever done in her life. Well, almost. A part of her whispered she should get back on that plane…he would never be any the wiser. And yet she couldn't, not now. The weight of the baby on her hip reminded her exactly why she'd come here.

She needed him to know. Needed to see his face. Get this whole thing off her conscience. And then she'd be done.

"Scusi."

The unfamiliar word reminded her that she was far from home.

"Sorry," she murmured, stepping aside to let the man pass. Unfortunately, he then held the door for her, forcing her to make a quick decision. Leave? Or stay?

Then she was through the door, the black marble floor as cold and hard as the words she'd said to a group of people at work thirteen months ago.

The man didn't rush off like she expected him to do, but said something else to her in Italian. She shook her head to indicate she didn't understand, shifting Annalisa a bit higher on her hip.

"English?" he asked.

"Yes, do you speak it?"

"Yes, can I help you find something?" He glanced at the baby and then back at her. "Are you a patient?"

"No, I'm looking for…"

Her eyes skated to the wall across from her,

where pictures of staff members were displayed along with their accreditation. And there he was: Hair as black as night. His eyes that were just as dark. But unlike the chilly floors beneath her feet, his had always been warm, flashing with humor. The eyes in the picture, however, were somber, the laugh lines that had once surrounded them barely noticeable.

Elyse swallowed. Had she done that to him?

Of course she had. But her back had been up against a wall. She'd had a choice to make. It had obviously been the wrong one.

She'd chosen the coward's way out. Just as she'd done nine months earlier. But she was here to make amends, if she could. Not in their relationship. That was certainly gone. Destroyed by her pride, her stupidity, and her fear of history repeating itself. But she could at least set one thing right. What he did with that information was up to him.

"You're looking for...?"

The man in front of her reminded her of her reason for coming.

What if he wasn't here yet? It was still early. Oh, he was here. He worked notoriously long hours. "I'm actually looking for an…old friend. He used to work at the same hospital that I did in the States."

"Luca?"

Relief swamped her. "Yes. Do you know where I can find him?"

He glanced at her, a slight frown marring his handsome face. "Refresh my *memoria*. Which hospital?"

"Atlanta Central Medical Center."

"Ah, I see." Something about the way he said it made her wonder exactly what Luca had said about his exit from the hospital. It didn't matter. Nothing he could have said would be worse than the truth. Although she hadn't orchestrated the layoffs, perhaps she also hadn't fought them as hard as she could have. At the time, a tiny part of her had wondered whether, if she and Luca weren't working together, it might be a way to repair some of the rifts that had been growing between them. Rifts she knew she had caused. But scars from a previous relationship had made her extremely wary of workplace romances.

And Luca hadn't been able to see how their dating could complicate their jobs, even after they'd erupted in a fierce argument during a meeting, disagreeing over the diagnosis of a patient and causing the whole room to stare at them. Kind of like this man was doing now.

"I'm sorry," he said, as if realizing his gaffe. "Come. I'll take you to Luca."

"Thank you. I'm Elyse Tenner, by the way." She shifted Anna yet again. She'd gotten her directions wrong, leaving the bus a few stops too early, and the heat was taking its toll on her. So much for going in looking cool and unruffled.

"Nice to meet you. I'm Lorenzo Giorgino. I work with Luca here at the clinic. I'm one of the neurosurgeons." He held out his arms. "Why don't you let me take her? You look tired."

Yet another blow to her confidence. But he was right. She was exhausted, both physically and emotionally. Between jet lag and the long walk, she could use a place to sit down.

She hesitated for a moment, then he said, "I promise not to break her. I have two...*nipoti*. What's your word for it? Nieces?"

Smiling, she held Anna out to him. She should have brought her baby sling, but she hadn't been able to think straight since the plane had touched down. Nerves. Fear.

Hadn't Luca told her he was in no hurry to have children? He had. More than once, in fact. She swallowed hard, even as this doctor's hands cradled the baby like an old pro, speaking to her in Italian.

He glanced at Elyse, just a hint of speculation in his eyes. "Ready?"

Not at all, but she wasn't going to make her confessions to anyone other than Luca himself. So she lied.

"I am. Lead the way." In handing Anna over, the die had been cast and her decision made. She was going to walk into Luca's office with her head held high and tell him that Anna was his daughter, and then hope that, in doing so, she'd made the right decision.

Luca stared at the EEG readings in front of him. Taken from a six-year-old boy, they showed the typical running waves of a Rolandic seizure. Benign. Filippo would more than likely outgrow them. Great news for his parents, who were worried out of their minds. It was always a relief to have a case where there was no threat to life. Just a temporary bump in the road.

Kind of like his time in the US had been. One big bump in the road, followed by a wave of smaller ones that still set him back on his ass at odd moments. But he thought it was getting better. His mind dwelt on her less. Or maybe it was just that he kept himself so busy that he didn't have time to think about her.

Kind of like he was doing now?

"Porca miseria!"

A second or two after the words left his mouth, there was a knock on the door to his office. Great. He hadn't mean to swear quite that loudly.

"Yes?"

Lorenzo appeared in the doorway, holding a baby.

Shock stilled his thoughts. "Everything okay?"

"Someone is here to see you."

It was obviously not the baby, so he raised his brows in question.

"She said she worked with you in Atlanta."

A section of his heart jolted before settling

back into rhythm. He'd worked with a lot of people at Atlanta Central.

"Does this person have a name?"

"I'd probably better let her tell you herself." Lorenzo switched to English.

This time the jolt was stronger. Lasted longer. Surely it wasn't… But the look on his friend's face told him all he needed to know.

He hadn't dated since he'd returned to Italy and didn't see himself doing so anytime in the near future. And those plans to revisit his decision to leave Atlanta permanently? Put off over and over until it was far too late to do anything about it.

He hadn't been able to stomach going back to his hospital in Rome either. His parents and two sisters lived there, and he hadn't felt like answering a million questions. Oh, there'd still been the worried texts and phone calls about why he'd suddenly returned to Italy, but since they hadn't been able to see his face, he was pretty sure he'd put their fears to rest. As far as they knew, he'd simply decided to practice in his own country. A short tenable statement. One he'd stuck to no matter how hard it was to force those words past his lips.

He ignored the churning in his stomach. "Okay, where is she?"

Instead of answering, Lorenzo pushed the door farther open and came into the room, revealing the woman who'd driven him out of the States and back to Italy.

Hell!

Chaotic memories gathered around, all of them pointing at the figure in front of them. He swallowed hard in an effort to push them back.

"Elyse? What are you doing here?" There was a slight accusation in his tone that he couldn't suppress. A defense mechanism, another way to hold back the wall of emotion.

Dio. He'd fallen for this woman, once upon a time, and then she'd gone and stabbed him in the back in the worst possible way. Better to let her know up front that he hadn't forgotten.

But why was she in Italy?

When she didn't answer, Lorenzo turned and handed her the baby. Shock flared up his spine. He looked from one to the other as a sudden horrible thought came to him. Did the two of them know each other? Was that why she'd made sure he was fired?

No. Of course not. Lorenzo had never been out of Italy as far as he knew. There was no way the two of them could have met.

"I'll go so you can talk." Lorenzo glanced at Elyse. "It was very nice meeting you."

"Thank you. You as well."

Then he backed out of the room and closed the door behind him with a quiet click.

Something in Luca's brain had frozen in place, the gears all stuck for several long seconds. His ass was also still firmly in his chair, something his mother would have frowned about.

But the memories were still doing their work, each one stabbing his heart and sticking there, like darts on a dartboard.

She ventured closer to the desk. "Luca?"

Somehow he dislodged his tongue, making a careful sidestep around the biggest question in his head while he puzzled through it. "How's your mother?"

He glanced at the baby. Elyse didn't have any siblings, so that wasn't a niece she was holding. Had she adopted a child after he'd left?

"She's still hanging in there. The Parkinson's progression has remained slower than average."

They'd tried an experimental treatment a few years back that had helped tremendously, even if it hadn't rolled back the clock.

"Good." Of course she hadn't traveled all this way just to report on her mother's condition. That left one question: Why was Elyse Tenner standing in the middle of his office, holding a baby? He nodded toward the seat in front of the desk. "Would you like a coffee?"

She sank into one of the chairs with what looked like relief. "I would love one, thank you."

"When did you arrive?" He got up and measured grounds into his coffee press and turned on the kettle to heat the water. The mindless task gave his fuzzy brain time to work through a few of the more obvious items: yes, she was really here, and he was pretty sure she wouldn't be if he'd simply left his toothbrush at her place. So it had to be something important. Important enough to travel across the ocean to see him.

His eyes went to the baby again before rejecting the thought outright. She would have told him before now.

"My flight arrived this morning."

"You have a hotel?"

And if she didn't? There was always his place. His thoughts ventured into dangerous territory.

Not happening, Luca.

He carried the pot with its water and coffee to the desk and set it down before retrieving two cups off the sideboard.

"Yes, I stopped at the hotel first, before coming here."

He poured the coffees and reached into the small fridge beside his desk, hiding his disappointment by concentrating on the mundane task before him. She'd always taken her coffee like he did, with a splash of milk. He added some to both, stirring a time or two before pushing one across toward her.

He studied her face. It was pale and drawn, her cheekbones a little more pronounced than they'd been a year earlier. "So what brings you to Italy?"

There was a marked hesitation before she

answered. "You, actually. I need to tell you something."

That jolt he'd experienced earlier turned into an earthquake, pushing all other thoughts from his head except for the one staring him in the face.

"You do?"

"Yes." Elyse slowly turned the baby to face him. "This is Annalisa." Her eyes closed, and her throat moved a time or two before she went on. "She's your—she's *our* daughter, Luca."

A hundred emotions marched across that gorgeous face over the course of the next few seconds, ranging from confusion to shock before finally settling on anger. His hands came together, fingers twining tightly, the knuckles going white. "My what?"

The words were dangerously soft.

He'd heard what she'd said. He just didn't believe it. And Elyse wondered for the thousandth time if it wouldn't have been better just to leave well enough alone. To raise Anna on her own and let Luca stay in the dark about his part in her existence. But she owned it to Annalisa and, if she was honest, to Luca himself, to own up to the circumstances behind their daughter's birth. If he rejected her claim outright, then at least she'd tried.

She probably should have tracked him down during her pregnancy, but it had been a difficult time. She'd been so caught up in grief over his leaving that she hadn't realized she was pregnant until she'd missed her third period. A test had revealed the worst. And she knew exactly when it had happened. That day in her office. The day he'd left the States forever.

She had been going to call and tell him, but each time she'd picked up the phone, she'd gotten cold feet, afraid that hearing his voice would undo any tiny bits of healing that had taken place. She'd kept telling herself she'd do it tomorrow. Except a month of tomorrows had gone by, and then things had suddenly started to go wrong with her pregnancy. She'd been placed on bed rest. Her parents had come to the house to help her. Her mom had been a trouper, despite her own medical issues. Elyse wasn't even sure the baby would survive at that point, so she'd elected to keep the news to herself in case the worse happened. And now she couldn't…would never be able to…

Annalisa was the only chance she would ever have to do this right. She swallowed back her fear.

"It's true, Luca. She's yours. I thought you should know." She settled the baby against her shoulder once again.

He swore. At least she thought it was a swear word, from his tone of voice.

God, she'd been right. He didn't want Anna. She'd been wrong to come. Wrong to tell him.

"You *kept* this from me? All this time? You come waltzing into my office with Lorenzo, who is holding a baby that I think is his niece?" He drew an audible breath. "Only he hands the baby to you. And now you tell me she's *mine*?"

Her chin went up in confusion. "It isn't like it was easy. You left, and you had no intention of coming back, isn't that right?"

"Yes."

"And didn't you insist more than once that you didn't want children?"

That had him sitting back in his chair, his eyes going to Anna. "I did, but that was—"

"I didn't think you'd even *want* to know."

"You didn't think I'd... *Mio Dio*. Well, you were wrong. And my statement about kids, if I remember right, included the phrase 'not right now.' The word 'never' was not mentioned. Ever."

How was she supposed to know that? There were men who would be just as happy to never father a child and who wouldn't want to know even if they did.

But as she'd taken that choice away from him, he had every right to be angry with her.

"I'm sorry. Things were tenuous at the time." She didn't go into the particulars of the precarious pregnancy or the fact that she would never give birth to another child. Anna might be his concern, but the other stuff? Not so much, since they were no longer a couple. And that fact hurt more than it should have, especially after all this time.

"Tenuous." His brows drew together. "*Tenuous?* You let a colleague of mine hold my child before I get a chance to, and that's all you can say?"

Yep, she was right. He was mad. Livid, even, and she couldn't blame him. She held Anna close against the tirade.

He noticed it, and his eyes closed. "Dammit, I'm sorry."

The sudden ache in her chest made her reach out and touch the edge of his desk with fingers that trembled.

"No, *I'm* sorry, Luca. It just never seemed like the right time and I couldn't... I didn't want to tell you over the phone." She didn't want to admit how afraid she'd been to hear his voice. And after Annalisa's birth she'd had a recovery period that most new mothers didn't have to worry about. It had delayed any travel plans she might have made. So here they were. In the present.

"When?"

She withdrew her hand. What was he asking? When Anna was born? When she was conceived? That was the kicker. They'd had sex in the aftermath of the announced downsizing, when there had been anger on both sides. Their coming together had been volatile and passionate. But the erotic coupling had solved nothing and only after her missed periods had she remembered that they hadn't used protection.

In the end, the layoffs that she'd hoped would save their relationship—by removing the work dynamics that had bothered her so much—had done the opposite. She hadn't wanted anyone to think she played favorites, and Luca had never asked for special treatment.

But memories of a former boyfriend's behavior had loitered in the background, ready to pounce, warning her of what had happened in the past. Of what could happen again if she weren't careful. Kyle had also been a colleague. He had asked—and expected—her to make allowances for things at work, most of them small and unimportant. But with each instance she'd gotten more and more uncomfortable with the relationship. Just as she'd been ready to break things off, he'd asked her to overlook a mistake he'd made with a patient. She hadn't, and he'd been fired.

She told herself she'd never put herself in that position ever again. Except then Luca had come along and all those warnings had been in vain.

Remembering his question, she decided on the simplest answer possible. If he wanted to do the math, he could. "Anna is four months old."

"Four months." He placed his hands flat on the desk. "I want to spend time with her. Did you come by yourself?"

He didn't ask if she was sure Anna was his.

A lump formed in her throat.

"And I want you to spend time with her. That's part of why I came. No, I didn't come alone. Peggy came with me. You remember my aunt?" If her mom had been well enough, Elyse would have asked her to come, but since she couldn't, this was the next best thing. She'd needed the moral support or she might have backed out entirely.

As many times as Luca had asked her out, she might have held firm to her resolve that there would be no more work relationships after Kyle. Until the day Luca had come out of one of the surgical suites after monitoring a patient's brain waves, white-faced, a grim look of defeat on his face. It had done her in.

She'd walked over to him, laid a hand on his arm and asked him out.

He'd said yes. The rest was history. A history peppered with moments of beauty and the sting of pain.

But the way he made love...

The realization that her eyes were tracking over his broad shoulders made her bite her lip and force herself to look away.

God! The attraction was still there—still very real. Even if the fairy tale had crashed to dust around her feet.

But from that rubble had come her baby girl. She would go through every bit of that pain all over again if she was the end result.

"After all this time, why come at all? You could have let things be. Never told me at all," Luca pressed.

The very things she'd told herself as she'd booked her flight.

"It was the right thing to do." Her hand went to Anna's head, rocking her subconsciously, still shielding her.

He looked at the baby for a second and walked over to the window, staring out, hands thrust in his pockets, shoulders hunched. "La *cosa giusta?* The right thing would have been to tell me long before she was born.

"Would it have changed things?"

He swung back around to face her. "I don't know. I wasn't given that choice, was I?"

"No." Maybe she needed to tell him at least a little of the circumstances. "When I said things were tenuous, I meant it. The doctors weren't sure Anna was going to make it for a while. And I didn't see any reason to say anything if…"

All the color drained out of his face, and he walked back to the desk. *Dio.* What happened? Is she okay?"

She rushed to put his mind at ease. "She's fine. Now. I had placenta previa. It didn't resolve and there were a couple of incidents of bleeding, heavy enough to cause worry." And in the end it had been life-threatening to both of them when it had ruptured. "I wasn't going to do anything that might put her at even more risk."

"And telling me would have done that?" He dragged a hand through his hair.

"I was talking more about physical stress but, yes. Inside I think I was afraid of jinxing the pregnancy. As if telling you might cause everything to fall apart, and I'd lose her. I didn't see any reason for us both to grieve if she didn't survive."

Not that she'd been sure he would. Because she'd convinced herself that he'd be horrified to have fathered a child in the first place.

"And after she was born? Why wait four months?"

She wasn't quite ready to share more than she already had.

"Does it really matter? I'm here now."

He crouched in front of her and touched the baby's arm with his index finger. "I can hardly believe she's mine."

"She is." She wasn't sure if he was questioning Anna's parentage, but either way she understood. Here came a woman who shows up over a year after they break up, claiming he'd fathered her child. "We can do a paternity test, if you want."

"No, I know she's mine." He looked up into her face. "Can I see her?"

She realized Anna was sound asleep, but the baby was still facing away from him. A tiny flutter of relief mixed with fear went through her midsection. While she hadn't thought Luca would reject his own daughter outright once he knew she existed, she hadn't been sure what his actual reaction would be.

She carefully turned the baby, cradling her in her arms so that he could see her tiny face. A muscle worked in his jaw and he stroked her hair. "How long are you here?"

"I have a little time left of my medical leave. I want you to get to know her. But…" she hesitated "…I want to have some ground rules in place. Come to an agreement first."

His fingers stilled. "The only agreement we need is that we have a child." There was a hard edge to his voice that told her he wasn't going to let her call all the shots here. And she wasn't trying to.

"I know that, Luca. I'm hoping we can——"

"A daughter. My daughter." The anger had melted away and in his voice was a sense of awe. "Annalisa."

A dangerous prickling behind her eyes made her sit up, teeth coming together in a way that forced it back.

"Yes."

His head came up. "I have a few ground

rules of my own. First we are going to figure out our schedules and come up with a plan."

His fingers flipped pages on his phone for a moment, probably looking at his caseload. "I have some free time right now, in fact. So I can drive you back to your hotel, and then we'll sit down and talk about any concerns you might have. But I want to make one thing perfectly clear. I *will* be a part of my daughter's life. No matter how much you might dislike me personally."

CHAPTER TWO

PEGGY SLIPPED OUT of the room as soon as the greetings were exchanged. She promised to be back in an hour.

A prearranged signal to keep Elyse from enduring his company?

His gut tightened in anger, even as his eyes soaked in the sight of his daughter. Now that the shock was wearing off, he could finally look beyond his own emotions and see Anna for who she was.

Unlike her *mamma*'s silky blond locks, which had always driven him to distraction, the baby's hair was black and thick and stuck up around her head at odd angles that made him smile. A red satin bow gathered one of the bunches onto the very top of her head, where it did a tiny loop-the-loop. As dark as her hair was, her skin was Elyse's through and through. It was as pale as the sand on the beaches of Sardinia. When she grew up, she'd probably blush just like her *mamma* too.

Cieli, he'd loved the way Elyse's cheeks had bloomed to life when he'd whispered to her at night. Realizing his gaze had moved from the baby to the green eyes of the woman holding her, he gave a half smile when color swooped into her face. Right on cue. Some things never changed.

And neither did his reaction to them.

Elyse cleared her throat and looked away, jiggling the baby in her arms. "So her full name is Annalisa Marie."

Maybe coming back to her hotel hadn't been such a good idea after all. But he'd wanted this discussion to happen in a more private setting. He didn't want Lorenzo or anyone walking in on them and asking questions before he had some answers.

"Marie. After your mother?"

Her attention turned back to him. "Yes."

He liked the nod to a woman he had come to admire in the few times they'd met, but there was also the sense of lost time…lost opportunities. He hadn't even been able to help choose his own child's name. Hadn't been there to see the first time she'd rolled over—if she had yet—and whatever other milestones four-month-olds normally achieved. "You gave her an Italian name."

"It was only right. She's half-Italian." She smiled, although there was an uncertainty to it. Had she honestly thought he wouldn't want his own child? Just because of some offhand comment he'd made? His reasons for saying it had had more to do with not scaring Elyse off—he hadn't wanted her to think he was rushing her to deepen their relationship. He did want kids. Just hadn't needed them right that second.

And now he had one. He was already in love, after only knowing her for an hour.

"Do you want to hold her?"

The question made him stop. Did he? His jaw tightened. Another thing he'd missed: holding her at birth.

He could worry about that later, though. Right now, he needed to concentrate on what was in front of him, not what was out of his control, as difficult as that might be.

And, yes, he wanted to hold her. He held out his arms and Elyse carefully placed their daughter in them. Looping an arm beneath her legs to support her, he held the baby against his chest, her baby scent tickling his nose. A sense of awe went through him.

He glanced at Elyse, who had taken a step back and stood watching them, arms wrapped tight around her midsection. There was a look on her face that he couldn't decipher. Despite the bitterness and chaos of their breakup thirteen months ago, he and Elyse had at least done something right. They'd made this tiny creature. Murmuring to her in Italian, so her *mamma* wouldn't understand, he turned and walked toward the hotel's window and looked out over the city.

"You don't know me yet, Annalisa, but I promise you will." Was that even realistic? How long was Elyse planning to be in Italy? She'd said she had a little medical leave left but hadn't specified how much.

When would she be back?

Bile washed up his throat when he thought of going months or a year between visits. But how could it be any different than that? Atlanta and Florence might as well be on separate planets.

He looked through the window at the city below. "This is part of your heritage, Anna. I want you to see Italy. To grow up speaking its language." He was going to make that happen, somehow.

A sound behind him made him look back. Elyse had moved to the front door, as if ready to push him out of his daughter's future before he'd even planted himself into her present. What he'd said was the truth, though. He was going to be a part of her life.

He could start by making sure they were all under the same roof for the duration of her stay. "You should come stay at the house, instead of at the hotel. I have some spare bedrooms. Your aunt will come as well, of course."

"I don't know." She bit her lip. "It might be better if we stayed here at the hotel."

"Why?"

He was already booked solid with appointments at the hospital for the next month. He couldn't just blow them all off and take a vacation. Especially not a couple of the patients who were set to undergo treatment in the coming days.

He crossed the room. "You've had Annalisa to yourself for four months. I'd like you to be there when I get home. When I get up."

Hell, was he talking about wanting Anna there? Or Elyse? He'd better make it clear. "I want as much time with her as possible. And there's a kitchen and more room to spread out than you have here. It'll make it easier on everyone."

"I don't…"

He shifted the baby into one arm, tilting Elyse's face with the crook of his index finger. "Say yes. It would mean a lot to me."

Something flickered through her green eyes before she said, "Are you sure? It'll be for a whole month."

A month. Said as if it were an eternity, when really it was only a millisecond. But at least now he knew how long he had with his baby.

"A month is nothing."

The weight of his daughter in his arms felt right. Good. He didn't want to give that up. Not in a month. Not in a year. Not in a lifetime.

With her head still tilted, they stared at each other.

"Is it?" Her words came out breathy, lips still slightly parted.

Damn. His midsection tightened in warning. A warning he ignored, leaning closer even as she seemed to stretch up toward him.

Annalisa chose that moment to squirm, and fidget, giving a soft cry. The spell was broken, and he stepped back.

"Sorry," she said. "She's getting hungry." The breathiness was gone, replaced by a wariness he didn't like.

He handed the baby over, watching as Elyse went to the bed and sat, unbuttoning her blouse and helping the baby latch on.

The fact that she did it right in front of him made the tenseness in his chest release its hold.

He'd been her lover, for God's sake. Why should he be surprised?

What did surprise him was that she'd come to Italy at all. Did she really care about him getting to know his daughter? Or was she simply assuaging any future guilt she might feel if Annalisa asked questions about who her father was?

Did it matter?

Yes, it did. Because her motivation behind this trip would set the tone for their future encounters. If she was just looking for the occasional photo op to show that she'd made the effort, she was going to be sorely disappointed. He wanted—no, he *intended*—to have an actual relationship with Anna. He would not be content with being the type of absentee father who did nothing more than send an occasional gift at birthdays or Christmas.

Adorable snuffling sounds came from the bed, where the baby still nursed. Suddenly he couldn't bear to watch anymore, looking on from the outside.

"I'm going down to get a drink. Do you want anything?"

Elyse looked up, the slight smile that had been on her lips fading. "A water, if it's not too much trouble?"

"No trouble at all."

A few steps later, he was opening the door, tossing one last look over his shoulder as he exited. But not before his eyes met hers and he saw the one thing he'd never wanted to see in them: fear. What was she afraid of? That he might try to take Annalisa away from her? He would never do that. But he also wasn't going to simply step back and pretend his child didn't exist.

The elevator ride gave him the little bit of space and time he needed. It unclogged the lump in his throat and eased the ache in his chest. At least for the moment.

She'd agreed to come to the house. That was something. She hadn't refused outright.

There was no sign of Peggy in the empty lobby where he asked for a coffee and Elyse's water. It made sense. The Peggy he'd known in the States was kind and considerate. She might make it a point to stay away for more than an hour, if she thought they needed the time to work out stuff with the baby.

Luca had juggled some of his calendar, but he still had appointments this afternoon, so he wouldn't be able to stay long as it was.

Dammit. He could just clear his calendar for the rest of the day—or a week, for that matter—but it wasn't fair to the clinic's patients. And even shuffling the cases to other neurophysiologists in the area would be a challenge. He was sure everyone else was just as slammed as he was. This was tourist season and a busy one for most of the doctors and clinicians in the city.

So what did he do?

All he could do. Make sure he used his time with Elyse and Annalisa wisely and hope that he could find a compromise that would suit all of them. She'd agreed to move into his house. They'd start with that.

Why had she agreed to stay at his home?

The expression on his face when he'd looked at her, that's why. The raw emotions that had streamed through her. The way he'd gripped his daughter tightly as if afraid to let her go. None of that fit with the man who'd said with such confidence that he didn't want children.

It was one of the million and one excuses she'd told herself every time she'd picked up the phone to call him and then set it back down again. She hadn't been sure how Luca would react to the news that he'd fathered a daughter, which was why she'd finally decided to come to Italy and look him in the eye. If he'd shown any hint of horror or rejection at the news, Elyse would have been devastated. She would have turned back around and caught the first flight out of Italy to save her daughter the pain of having a father who didn't want her.

But he hadn't rejected her, had insisted he wanted to be a part of her life. The distance between Italy and her homeland was going to make that extremely hard.

If he were still in Atlanta, it would have been so much easier.

Would it have been?

It wasn't like she'd could have hidden the weight gain from him. He'd have known. Plus the added stress of having him right there might have made an already difficult pregnancy worse.

And knowing Anna was going to be her only child?

None of this was easy, and having him stand there as she'd nursed had driven that point home. It was a relief to have him leave. It gave her enough time to finish up, since Annalisa was barely hanging on, her long dark lashes fluttering as she got sleepy.

Moving the baby to the crook of her arm, she quickly closed herself back up before lifting the baby to her chest and gently rubbing her back until she burped. And a good burp it was too. Elyse chuckled and got up to put the baby in the portable crib she'd brought on the flight with her.

Anna shifted in her sleep, raising small fists that slowly floated back down until they were at her sides.

Wow. She could stare at her daughter all day long. There were times she found herself forgetting what she was supposed to be doing because of it. Once she started back at the hospital, that would all change and life would become chaotic once again.

One month. That's all she had left.

She didn't want to think about how long it would be until Luca could see Anna again. Elyse would be able to follow the minuscule day-to-day developments of their daughter's personality and physical growth.

He would miss out on so much.

But she didn't know how to make it better.

Maybe he could move back to the States.

And do what? Her hospital's neurology department was still operating on a skeleton crew and they weren't looking to expand that area. But there were other hospitals and other clinics. Surely he could find a place at one of those, just like she'd thought he would do all those months ago.

Why would he, though? She'd been awe-struck at the little bit of Florence she'd seen as she'd come in. The city was gorgeous, with true old-world charm that couldn't be matched. The Florence Cathedral and its domed roof was one of the most beautiful buildings she'd seen in her life. She needed to make a point to get a closer look at it. Then there was the Pitti Palace and so many other historic sites that she wanted to explore. Maybe while Luca was at the hospital, working, she, Peg and the baby could do some sightseeing.

After seeing where he came from, she couldn't imagine him wanting to move back to Atlanta. But maybe the baby would change that.

Did she want it to? It was hard seeing him again. The punch to her senses had been just as jolting as the first time she'd laid eyes on him. And when he'd tipped up her face... God. For a second, she had been sure he was going to kiss her. Had wanted him to so badly.

How much worse would that be if they lived a half-hour apart? Or maybe even closer than that? Or saw each other every day? She was obviously not as over him as she'd thought.

There was a quiet knock at the door and then Luca came in, holding a coffee in one hand and a water in the other. Suddenly she was wishing she'd asked for one of those instead of the water. "Thank you," she said as she took the bottle, her eyes still on his cup.

He must have noticed her wistful gaze because he said, "Did you want coffee?"

"No. It's okay. I'll just have water." She uncapped her bottle and took a quick slug, the cold liquid making her stomach clench as it hit. She couldn't repress the slight grimace. She drank water because it was good for her, but it had never been her favorite beverage.

"Are you sure you don't want some? It has milk. Just like you like."

Something about that sent a rush of moisture to her eyes. She wasn't even sure why. He'd given her coffee in his office too. It had to be the stress of the trip and everything that went with it. Before she could stop herself, she blurted out, "Could I? Just a sip."

"You're the one who introduced me to milk in my coffee." He smiled and handed her the cup, the heat of it in her hands a welcome change from the incessant blowing of the air conditioner. She took a tiny sip.

Oh! That was good. Rich and dark and full of flavor. She took a second sip and then a third before finally forcing herself to hand the cup back.

"Are you sure you don't want more?"

"Positive. But that was delicious."

He smiled. "Italian. Hard to beat."

Yes, it was. And not just the coffee. She'd missed him. Missed the good times. The love-making. The laughter. But she didn't miss what had come toward the end. That huge fight during the meeting about the patient's diagnosis had caused a major rift between them. Add that to her growing uneasiness about their relationship, her fear that she would repeat the mistakes she'd made with Kyle. And then the final blow of the downsizing. She hadn't even been able to warn Luca about it before it happened due to that same fear of showing him preferential treatment.

It was easier with him gone. She kept telling

herself that, even though easier didn't necessarily mean better. It was just less complicated.

Less complicated? Was she kidding? They had a baby now. She shook that thought away, washing the coffee down with another sip of water, as if that would take care of the predicament she found herself in. If she'd had an abortion she wouldn't be here right now.

And yet... Her eyes went to the baby's crib. There's no way she'd give any of this up, even if she could.

"Remind me to buy some Italian roast coffee before I go back to the States."

"It won't be the same as drinking it here."

No, it wouldn't. Life itself wasn't the same since he'd left. But he'd made it pretty obvious back then that he wasn't interested in working things out.

Maybe they'd been similar in all the wrong ways. They were both neurologists, even if their respective specialties had subtle differences to them. Elyse treated patients, and while Luca dealt with patients as well, his side was more involved in testing, interpreting and diagnosing. But the two subspecialties overlapped. A lot. And there had been times she'd been certain of a diagnosis and had spoken her mind. Luca had never challenged her.

Until that one difficult case, when he'd done so during a staff meeting. If he'd been a nurse, a tech, or even another doctor, it might have been a nonissue. She could have listened and then made a decision based on the evidence at hand. That would have been that. But because it was Luca, she'd found herself wanting to defer to him. Not because she thought he was necessarily right but because of their relationship. And she knew herself well enough to know it would happen again. Why? Because she'd been there once before with Kyle.

If she and Luca had worked at different hospitals, those murky situations wouldn't have arisen in the first place. They could have....

She sighed, cutting herself off. All the might-haves in the world wouldn't change the reality of what was. Or the fact that he'd clearly found it easy to leave Atlanta—and her—behind.

Luca sat in one of the two club chairs in the room, backed by a wall that was thickly textured, like those in many of the buildings she'd seen. Elyse perched on the edge of one of the two beds. Thank goodness the maid service had already been and tidied up. It might have made an already awkward situation even more unbearable.

Elyse decided to tackle the elephant in the room. "So where do we go from here, Luca?"

"I don't know." He glanced at the crib, where the baby was currently sleeping. "Right now I'm wishing I had more than a month with her."

"I know. I wish you did too. But my maternity leave is going to end. I don't see how I can extend it." She didn't add that she hadn't been sure of his reaction.

The fact that he was sitting here saying he wanted more time with Anna created an entirely different problem.

She went on. "If you have any ideas—other than my leaving her behind—I'm open to suggestions." She hadn't meant it as a jab at the past, but the quick tightening of his lips said he'd taken it as one.

"I would never ask you to leave her."

"I know that."

His elbows landed on his knees, hands dangling between his strong thighs. Thighs that she'd once…

Nope. No going down that path, Elyse. That's what had gotten her in trouble in the first place.

Luca had captured her attention from the moment he'd walked onto her floor at the hospital. Only she had just gotten out of a difficult relationship with Kyle a year earlier and hadn't been anxious to repeat the experience. She'd resisted going out with him, feeling proud of herself, until he'd walked out of that surgical suite that day looking like a beaten man. He'd touched her heart, and the rest was history. She'd told herself the attraction would eventually burn itself out. It hadn't.

Even now, she knew she still wanted him.

He looked up. "I think we're overlooking the obvious solution."

Her heart leaped in her chest. Was he saying he wanted to get back together?

And if he did?

She swallowed. He lived here, and she lived in Atlanta. Besides, the damage had been done. He'd never forgive her for firing him. He'd made that pretty clear when he'd left.

"I guess I'm still overlooking it, because I don't see an obvious solution at all."

"We could get married."

Her mouth, which had been open to make a completely different suggestion, snapped shut again. Surely she hadn't heard him correctly?

"I'm sorry?" Maybe he *was* saying he wanted to get back together. But marriage? Um, no. Not a possibility.

She hurried to send the conversation in a completely different direction. "Maybe you could just move back to the States? We could work out an agreement for visitation."

Why had she said that? Maybe because that was the only obvious thing her brain could catch hold of. They could work at different hospitals and be aloofly friendly. Like those famous divorced couples who managed to get along for the sake of their kids.

"That's not quite what I had in mind."

"I can't marry you. We don't even like each other anymore." She forced out the words, even though they were a lie. She did like him. A little too much, in fact.

"You can't marry me? Or you won't?" Luca got up from his chair and went over to stand by the crib. He leaned over, fingers sliding over the baby's forehead, pushing back some dark locks of hair. Then he twirled the tiny ponytail in a way that made her stomach clench. Watching him with their baby girl set up an ache she couldn't banish.

It wasn't something she was likely to see every day as Annalisa grew up. But she couldn't marry him. Aside from the fact that he didn't love her—he'd as much as said so by not challenging her comment that they didn't even like each other—she couldn't have any more children. She had barely had time to grieve over that fact herself, much less tell anyone else.

Lord, she shouldn't have come here.

"Both. Getting married just because of Anna would be wrong. And not fair to either of us."

He turned to face her with a frown. "Is there someone else?"

"What? No, of course not." She gave a nervous laugh. "I've just had a baby. There's no time for romance."

"But there would be if the timing were better?"

"That's not what I'm saying."

"Well, I can't move back to the States right now. Not with my caseload."

Disappointment winged through her even though she knew he was right. He couldn't just pick up and leave at a moment's notice.

"It was just a suggestion."

He looked up, his gaze holding hers in a way that made her swallow. "You're currently on maternity leave. No patients or boyfriends waiting in the wings, right?"

Something began unfurling inside of her. Something she hadn't thought about. Something she hadn't even wanted to think about. Was he going to ask her to marry him again? If so, would she be able to resist?

"No, but the no-patients thing is only for a month, and then I have to be back."

"What if you didn't?"

"Sorry?"

"What if you didn't go? Instead of me moving to the States, what if you stayed here—in Italy—instead?"

CHAPTER THREE

PEG ARRIVED BEFORE Elyse could give him an answer to the staying-in-Italy question.

But the look of horror on his ex's face said that marriage was off the table. For good. He wasn't even sure why he'd asked that. It had just come to him as the easiest solution as he'd stood over his daughter's crib. But Elyse had made it clear that the chances of a marriage between them working were just about nil: they didn't even like each other. He could only assume she was speaking for herself.

Although he hadn't liked her very much either when she'd kicked him and the others out of their jobs. But after arriving back in Italy, he'd been the one doing the kicking…and it was his own behind. He should have stayed and finished that last fateful conversation—even if it had only been to gain closure. But he'd been so hurt and utterly furious that he couldn't have found the words in English to express any of it.

"Everything okay?" Peg looked from one to the other, a worried expression on her face.

Her niece gave her a smile that didn't quite reach her eyes. "Great."

It wasn't great. It was frustrating. He felt totally impotent to change things right now. But he was going to. Was going to fight, if necessary, to be involved in his daughter's life. Elyse marrying him would have made sure that happened. Maybe she was right to refuse. Kids were pretty intuitive nowadays. AnnaLisa would have eventually seen right through the sham, setting them up for a messy divorce down the road.

So no tying the knot. But surely they could live in the same vicinity. Or at least the same country. If she could put off going back to work for three months or maybe even six, he might be able to swing moving back to the US. Even if that prospect didn't thrill him like it once had.

Only with Elyse explaining to Peggy that they were going to be staying at his house, the chance to talk about things was gone. For now. He'd just have to pull her aside or sit them down when they didn't have an audience and hash it out.

And afterward? If she agreed to stay in Italy? She would have to remain in his house for the duration, because she wouldn't be able to afford a villa or even an apartment without working.

Luca wasn't at all sure how he felt about that. Especially after the way he'd reacted to her a few minutes ago.

He scribbled down the address and handed it to Elyse. "Just ask a cab to take you to this address. I'll let my housekeeper know to get a couple of rooms ready."

"Housekeeper?"

The way she said the word made him uneasy. "Emilia. She doesn't live there. Just comes during the week to clean the place up. Today happens to be one of those days. She won't mind. And she normally fixes a couple of meals and puts them in the fridge for me. There's a ton of food, so don't worry about cooking."

"That was part of the reason you wanted us

to stay at your place, though, because you had a kitchen we could use."

He smiled. She'd caught him. "I said you could use it, but I didn't say you had to cook in it."

"No, you didn't."

But her voice said she was beginning to have some misgivings, so maybe it was time to make himself scarce before she changed her mind. She'd already turned down his proposal of marriage, he didn't want her backing out of anything else. "I would go with you, but I have a patient scheduled in half an hour."

Peg spoke up. "We'll be fine. And thank you for letting us stay in your house. It will be a lot more comfortable for the baby than the hotel...won't it, Elyse?"

"Yes. Thank you."

The prodding and the reluctance of Elyse's response made his smile widen. He had an odd ally in Peggy, but if it got him closer to his goal—having his daughter within reach— it was worth it.

"I should be home before dinner. Just rest.

The recovery time for jet lag is one day per hour of time difference."

"In that case, we'll be well recovered by the time…"

She let the sentence trail away, and he wasn't sure if that was a good thing or a bad thing. Was she thinking about staying longer than a month? Or warning him that she would soon be leaving?

He was sure she and Peggy were going to have quite a discussion once he walked out of that door. Going over to the crib one last time, he murmured to Annalisa, telling her he would see her in a few hours. And hopefully his time with her would be measured in years, rather than just a few short weeks.

"Mary Landers, aged forty-three, a tourist from the US who has been having seizures over the last two weeks. She's in the MRI machine right now. The team could use a second look."

The receptionist at the front desk had already alerted him of that fact when he'd arrived. But his favorite nurse always liked to chat for a minute. His scheduled patient had already been advised that he'd be a few minutes late.

"I'll head up there now. Anything else I should know?"

With her silvery hair and friendly personality, he and Thirza had hit it off immediately. He could count on her to give him additional information on patients if he needed it, rather than having to look things up in the system. The fact that she had an eidetic memory was a great asset for the clinic.

"She got a workup at one of the neighboring hospitals and they suspected a brain tumor because of the cluster of symptoms that came with the seizures, but their scan didn't turn up anything concrete. They've added contrast to the one done here, hoping to get a better view of the way the vessels are laid out."

"Do you remember the cluster of symptoms?"

She brandished a slip of paper and a smile. "Of course. I wrote them down for you."

"*Grazie.*"

He was glad of the work. It would take his mind off the fact that he would once again be living with Elyse. Only temporarily, though, and he'd decided that was a good thing. Elyse was right. Marriage would have been a mistake.

Going up the stairs, because waiting for the elevator had never been his style, he exited through the door on the third floor and went to the imaging section. Once there, he used his passkey to get into the observation area.

"Luca, glad to see you. We still have about ten minutes before the scan is finished."

"Where's Lorenzo?"

"He's in surgery. He'll be down as soon as he finishes up."

The city of Florence was a tourist magnet, and they treated people of many nationalities. It helped that several of the doctors at the clinic spoke English with varying degrees of fluency. Faster communication meant faster treatment.

He glanced down at the paper in his hand: Seizures, double vision in the left eye, tremor on that same side, muscle weakness. He could see why the other clinic had initially thought she had a brain tumor. They did present with similar symptoms.

"Hey! Stop!" One of the techs was staring down at the patient. "She's seizing!"

The whole room went into action. They retracted the sliding table from the imager, while multiple staff members rushed into the room. Thank God they didn't allow family to observe the procedures.

A few minutes later, after administering an injection of lorazepam, they were able to stabilize her. She slowly regained consciousness, totally unaware of what had happened. She remembered a momentary sense of confusion just before the seizure hit.

Luca frowned. "How close were we to getting those scans finished?"

"About seven minutes."

"Before putting her back in the tube, let me look at what you have. Maybe we won't have to finish it."

Going back into the control room, they scrolled through the scans, the contrast agent helping to visualize blood vessels.

Dannazione! Everything looked pretty normal.

Wait.

"Can we replay those last images?"

The tech backed the slides up and slowly went through them again.

"There." He tapped a pen to the screen where a small, hyper-dense lesion nestled in the left ventricle. "See that?"

"I do. And I can understand how the other hospital missed it. Cavernoma?"

"It looks that way."

A cavernous malformation wasn't like an arteriovenous malformation, where the high pressure in the vessels put the patient at risk of a stroke or brain bleed. Cavernomas were normally asymptomatic, in fact. But since this patient had presented with both seizures and neurological deficits, the cavernoma was probably the cause and would have to be treated.

The problem was, the ventricles were deep in the brain and traditional microsurgery in those areas didn't always go well.

Elyse would love to sit in on this case.

Maybe she could. And it might be a way to coax her into staying longer. There was no reason she couldn't observe or weigh in with an opinion, was there? As long as she wasn't actually treating the patient, it should be fine.

"What do you think Dr. Giorgino will want to do?"

"I think he'll want to do a combined approach. Ventriculoscopy followed by microsurgery."

"Tricky," said the tech.

"Yes, but by getting an actual look at it, rather than just an MRI image, there's a better chance of success. I saw one of them done when I was in the States." It had actually been one of Elyse's patients. She'd performed the surgery and successfully removed the cavernoma. As far as he knew, the patient's symptoms had completely subsided afterward. "I actually know someone who's done a resection of one of these. I'll put her in contact with Lorenzo."

Again.

Lorenzo Giorgino—the good-looking man who'd held Anna in his office—was one of the top neurosurgeons in Italy. And he actually welcomed outside advice, unlike some specialists. Hopefully Elyse would be willing to help. She could even consult over the phone if she didn't want to actually come in to the clinic.

A little whisper at the back of his brain questioned whether that was a good idea. He'd had a visceral reaction when he'd found out the baby in Lorenzo's arms was actually his own daughter.

But they were all grown-ups. He could handle it.

Luca let the team know they'd found the problem and didn't need to put the patient through another round in the MRI machine. It would be up to Lorenzo and some other specialists to recommend treatment to control her symptoms until a surgery date could be set. The sooner the better.

As soon as that was resolved, he moved on to see the rest of his patients, putting Elyse, Lorenzo and everyone else out of his mind.

"Of course I'll help. I'd love to look at the scans."

Elyse was surprised that Luca had asked her to consult on a case after what had happened in Atlanta.

But this was Italy, not Atlanta. She was no longer the one in charge of his department. She was on Luca's turf now.

"I remembered the cavernoma case you had. The patient had a really good outcome, if I remember right."

"Yes, she's had no more problems since. It was in the right lateral ventricle rather than the left, but the procedure would be the same. You have a neurosurgeon who can perform it?"

She and Peg had moved into the house that afternoon. Her aunt loved it. She'd taken Annalisa into the garden to explore while Elyse had curled up on the couch with a magazine, which was where Luca had found her.

Even his housekeeper had left for the day. And meeting her had turned out to be a lot less awkward than Elyse had expected it to be. She wasn't sure if the woman knew the exact circumstances surrounding her sudden arrival, but it had to be pretty obvious. A woman shows up at her boss's door with a baby in tow…it didn't take a genius to figure it out. Emilia had eyed her daughter with interest, but the kindness behind the glance had prevented Elyse from bristling.

"We do. It's actually the doctor who brought you up to my office yesterday. I don't know how many, if any, of these he's done, but he's an excellent surgeon. One of the best."

"If he's careful and really pays attention to where he is at any given second, he should be fine."

"Which is why I wondered if you'd speak with him and compare notes. He's a good guy, I'm sure he'd be amenable."

"He seemed nice. I'll need to talk to Peg and see if she's okay with me going, but it sounds fascinating. And much better than lying around your pool all day, nice though that is."

He smiled, coming over to sit on one of the chairs flanking the couch. "You could always treat this like a vacation. Where's Annalisa, anyway?"

"She's in the garden with Peg. She should be in any moment. Whatever your housekeeper left in the oven smells divine, by the way. I could get a little too used to this." Then realizing he could take that as agreement to his marriage proposal, she added, "At least for this month. I haven't decided on moving to Italy, though, Luca. I'm not sure I'm ready to leave my job. I don't even know what I would do here."

"It wouldn't be forever. Could you at least ask for your leave of absence to be extended? Just long enough for us to think things through properly. I don't want either of us to feel rushed and then later be unhappy with the decisions made."

He'd done that exact thing once. Only there was no hint that he was unhappy with that decision.

He was right. A month was a very short time to come up with a plan for a lifetime.

"I don't know if they'll let me. I have a contract that spells things out." What if they decided to let her go just like they had Luca and the rest of them?

Well, her former colleagues had all bounced back, from what she'd heard from various sources. Surely she would too, if it came to that. She was pretty sure any of the larger hospitals in Atlanta would welcome her on board. She just wasn't sure she would welcome them. She'd been at Atlanta Central Medical Center ever since she'd graduated from med school. She didn't know anyplace else.

That fact may have led her to make her own rash decisions. Like staying on at the hospital instead of walking out with her team in protest at the firings. Everything had happened so fast she'd had no time to digest what it really meant to her.

She set aside the magazine she had been looking through when Luca leaned forward.

"Will you at least try? Ask them and see if it's a possibility? If it's not, and you're not willing to quit, then we have some things that need to be done quickly. Like getting my name added to her birth certificate."

A zip of shock went through her. Oh, Lord, she hadn't even thought about that. Hadn't thought about much other than informing him that he had a daughter. And now when she thought about it, that had been a pretty cold-blooded way to go about it. This was his child and yet in her head she'd made it into a mere formality, like a business letter: *We would like to inform you that...*

Annalisa was anything but business-oriented. She was a living, breathing human being who had a mother...*and* a father. To make it about anything else would be criminal. Maybe marrying him wouldn't have been as big a stretch as she'd made it out to be. It would make officially naming him as Anna's father easier.

Her heart cramped. But to marry him for anything other than love… She couldn't do it. She wasn't sure how to add him to Annalisa's birth certificate, or if they could even do it from Italy. He was right. She needed to at least ask the hospital for more time off. If they said no, her decision was made. But if they said yes…then she had some decisions of her own to make. And quickly.

"I'll call the hospital tomorrow morning and get the lay of the land."

"The lay of…?"

"Sorry. It means see if they're agreeable to an extension."

His English was so good it was easy to forget that it wasn't his native tongue. Some of the expressions didn't make much sense when you dissected them. That was another thing. He spoke excellent English, but her Italian was limited to what she'd learned from Luca and some of that made her blush. Not exactly the kind of talk that occurred around the dinner table. In fact, she could feel her face heat at the memory of some of those desperate phrases muttered in the heat of passion.

She hurried to ask, "Lorenzo speaks English pretty well, if I remember right."

"Yes. Most of the staff have some understanding of English. Anything you or they don't understand, I can translate."

"Thank you. If Atlanta does give me additional time off, I think I'd like to take a language course, if I can have Annalisa there with me."

"If you can't, I'm sure Emilia would love to watch her. Or I could set up a portable crib at the clinic and have her there. With me."

She opened her mouth to argue with him, but then snapped it shut when she remembered she'd already had four months to get to know her daughter. He'd had under a day to adjust to the fact that he was a father. Guilt pressed hard against her chest, making it difficult to breathe.

She uncurled her legs and leaned forward to take one of his hands.

"I'm really sorry, Luca. I should have found a way to get word to you. I just didn't know if she was even going to—"

"You're here now. Let's just leave it at that." Something in his eyes flashed, though, making her wonder if he was really that quick to forgive her.

She let go of his hand, stung by the coolness of his voice. Especially after the way the slide of her palm against his had awakened nerve endings that had gone into hibernation. It had been a long, cold season and there was no end in sight.

Who could blame him if he hated her? She hadn't been that quick to forgive herself. But how much worse would it have been if Anra had gone looking for her father once she reached adulthood and he'd found out about it then? Now, that would have been unforgivable. And both Annalisa and Luca would have missed out on some precious memories.

In the end, she'd done the right thing. Even if it wasn't the easy thing.

"Okay." The whispered word took a while to get out. "I don't know what else to say."

"I know this has been hard on you as well." His gaze softened. "I'm glad you came. Really glad."

With his black hair and dark eyes, he'd been

the epitome of tall, dark and mysterious. And with the difference in cultures, his body language wasn't as easy to pick up on as American men's were. Maybe that's why she'd been so drawn to him, even as she'd tried so hard to keep her distance. Unlike her, though, he'd let his feelings come through loud and clear from the very beginning, making her sizzle inside.

That had been wildly attractive. Looking back, it had only been a matter of time before she gave in. Only she'd never expected to be the one doing the asking. But she had. It had seemed inevitable at the time, though.

Luca knew what he wanted and set out to get it. Not something she was used to in the men she'd known. Not even Kyle had been so driven. Getting swept off her feet had been a heady experience.

She just had to be careful that she didn't let his charm affect her all over again or influence her in certain areas of her life. Like talking her into a sham marriage. For a second or two, the word "yes" had teetered on the tip of her tongue. But down that road lay craziness. Even if it had been for *their* daughter. A fact she had to remind herself of several times a day. She was no longer calling all the shots when it came to making decisions about Anna.

Before she could think of anything else to say, he stood and reached down his hand. "You must be hungry. And tired."

From her position her eyes had to skim up his body to get to his face. Heat flared as her glance swept over parts she'd once known in all their glory.

If it had been anyone else, she might have thought he was standing over her to intimidate her, to make himself look bigger and stronger, but she knew that wasn't how he operated. And other countries didn't have the same bubble of personal space that Americans did. At least, that's what she'd learned from Luca. He tended to stand close. To kiss close. To love close.

Elyse closed her eyes for a second before forcing herself to nod in the hope that he'd take a step backward, so she could stand as well. He must have read her mind, because he did just that, the hand he'd held down toward her dragged through his hair instead. He took a second step back. She climbed to her feet, only to discover that he was still well within her personal space. And with the couch behind her, she had nowhere to go.

His finger lifted to touch her cheek in a way that sent a shiver over her. "We're going to figure this out, Elyse. I promise."

Figure what out? How to kill the emotions swirling inside her that just would not die? Because his touch and the low rasp of his voice were doing just the opposite.

"I hope so."

Just then she heard the back door open and Peg's voice as she chattered to Annalisa.

"Perfect timing all around," he said, moving away from her.

"Yes, it is." Elyse smoothed her shirt down over her skirt with trembling hands, anxious to hide the turmoil whipping through her. She'd hoped all of those odd pangs of need for him would go away with time. And they had faded somewhat, but his presence had evidently popped a trapped bubble of longing, because a stream of it was hitting her system hard. So hard it was difficult to concentrate on anything but the way he looked, his scent, the way she'd once felt in his arms.

Staying at his house, for a week much less a month, was such a big mistake. She hurried over to Peg and lifted Annalisa out of her arms, hugging the baby to her.

Luca came over and chose that moment to kiss his daughter on the cheek, and when he looked up, they were inches apart, his lips heartbreakingly close. And there it was again. That quivery sensation she'd had a minute ago. Then he pulled back, with a smile that was full of hidden knowledge.

He knew exactly what he did to her.

"I'll go get check on dinner," he murmured, and then he was gone.

Her aunt glanced at her, eyes wide. Elyse wasn't the only one who'd noticed the disruption in the space/time continuum.

"Oh, my," she said, "I think I'll go help him. Annalisa is probably hungry for her dinner as well. She was getting a little fussy outside. Looks like I picked the wrong moment to come in."

"Oh, no, Peg. You picked the perfect time, believe me."

"I'm not so sure..."

But Anna *was* fussy again, starting to shift

and snort. The precursor to a complete melt-down. The baby wasn't the only one close to a meltdown. She could feel one coming on herself. She threw her aunt a grateful smile.

"Thanks, I'll feed her and put her down for a nap, so we can eat in peace."

Peace? Ha! Not much hope of that. Not as long as Luca was around.

Well, she was going to have to figure out how to deal with him before she did some-thing completely stupid.

Like fall for him all over again.

CHAPTER FOUR

"I DON'T KNOW, Elyse, we were counting on having you back on time. Isn't there any way you can keep to your original schedule?"

Not the words Elyse was hoping to hear this early in the morning. She'd dragged herself out of bed, nursed the baby, stuffed her feet into flip-flops and made her way out of the bedroom. Annalisa had gone back to sleep as soon as she was full.

As it was so early, she'd decided to get the thing she dreaded most out of the way. She called the hospital and reached the administrator. He was not overly accommodating, which was normal. She should be happy he was being difficult, that she would have an excuse to leave when her month was over but, oddly enough, she wasn't.

She couldn't blame him. It had been several months already. Her complicated pregnancy had meant not working as many hours as she'd used to. And then she'd been put on complete bed rest. No more patients, no more going into work. At all.

"I'll do my best. I'll let you know in a few days what I've decided." She thanked him and hung up the phone.

The longer she was here, the more complicated things promised to get with Luca. Surely whatever they had to work out could be done in a month. And he'd talked about maybe moving back to the States once his patient load was redistributed, in about six months' time.

Elyse swallowed. In six months Annalisa would be crawling and doing all kinds of other things. And Luca would miss all of it.

How was that fair? But how was staying here for six months fair to her? She would probably have to quit her job, put her career on hold in order to stay. And then there was her mom. Where would she be in six months? Yes, she had her younger sister Peg, her husband and a multitude of friends she could call on. But she only had one daughter: Elyse. And she would only ever have one grandchild.

There was no good solution. Something she'd told herself all day yesterday. They were going to have to come up with some kind of plan, though. And she knew that "plan" needed to include having Anna's father in her life.

That little act of fertilizing an egg had bound them together for life in some way, shape or form. That had been the easy part. The fun part. She shivered; yes, it had been a lot of fun.

Oh, there was fun in raising a child too, but it was definitely life-altering, in more ways than one. Luca would find out the reality of that soon enough. Like giving up months of a career that had taken years to build. He'd told her he couldn't move back to the States because of his patient load and had asked her to move to Italy instead. The problem was, he'd already practiced medicine in Atlanta, so he could take up where he'd left off with his career, whereas she...

She would have to give up everything she'd worked for. Scrabble up the ladder all over again.

Wasn't Anna worth it? Absolutely. But if

there was a better solution, she wanted to find it. And that meant some give-and-take on both their parts.

That would be something else they'd have to talk about. She didn't want to scare him, but she also didn't want him to just sit back and be content with coming over and kissing his daughter's cheek periodically. Annalisa's view of men was being formed with each interaction. It was up to both of them to make sure those interactions were meaningful and healthy.

She glanced down the hallway. Peggy was awake, evidently. Her bedroom door was open and when she made her way over there, there was no sign of her. Anna was still sound asleep. She padded to the kitchen, where she found her aunt chatting with Emilia, who was poised to crack an egg on the edge of a bowl.

"Good, you're awake. We were just talking about how you like your eggs." Peggy turned her head and mouthed, Oh, my God.

Elyse forced back a laugh. Her aunt wasn't used to having things done for her. She preferred to wait on people, not the other way around. "You don't have to cook for us,

Emilia. We know how to make eggs." She said the words in rapid English before pulling herself up short and slowing way down. "I'm sorry. Did you understand?"

"Yes. I like cook," Emilia replied with a smile.

Hoping Peggy wouldn't jump in and try to take over, she pronounced each word carefully. "Thank you. And I like eggs...scrambled?" She made a stirring motion with her hand, hoping to get across the meaning.

"Why are you talking like that?" Peg asked.

"What do you mean?"

She laughed. "One of Emilia's kids is studying English in the States. She understands quite a bit, she just doesn't like to speak it because she's afraid of making mistakes."

The housekeeper nodded as if in agreement.

Well, Emilia wasn't the only one afraid of making mistakes. Elyse was too. And not just with regard to the language. She was afraid of making a terrible mistake with her daughter or with Luca. One she'd have a hard time recovering from.

Don't hurt either one of them, Elyse.

The thought came unbidden and was unwelcome. She wouldn't if she could help it. Right now she was doing the best she could with what she had.

While Emilia cooked their breakfast, Peg motioned her into the other room. "You're going to the hospital to consult on a case this morning?"

Luca must have told her.

"Exactly how long have you been up?"

"Long enough to sit and have a chat with him." She squeezed her niece's hand. "He wants a relationship with her, honey. You need to give him a chance."

She frowned. "That's why we came here. To tell him about her."

"That's not what I mean, and you know it. He told me he asked you to stay in Italy, but that you weren't sure."

"Did he also tell you he asked me to marry him?"

"He what?" Her eyes went round with surprise. "What did you say?"

Elyse grimaced. "What do you think I said? No, of course. It was an impulsive suggestion. He didn't mean it."

"Are you sure?"

"Very sure. And as for staying, I just don't know how that would work. My administrator basically said he wants me back at the end of a month."

"Are you going to go? This is Anna's future we're talking about."

Elyse looked off into the distance for a moment. "I know. He hurt me, Peg."

"Are you so sure that was a one-way street? He lost his job, and you were the one who told him. You don't think that hurt *him*?"

"I had no choice about him losing his job. And I felt it was better coming from me than from a hospital bureaucrat."

"I'm not saying what you did was wrong. But it still had to sting."

She shrugged. "He left. Packed up his bags and was gone soon after the announcement."

"And you're afraid he'll do the same to Annalisa? He won't, you know he won't." Peg tilted her head. "Anna is a part of him. They'll always have that connection, no matter what his relationship with you is like."

Something burned behind her eyes. What Peggy said was true. That even if Elyse meant nothing to him, he would always love their daughter.

"You're right as usual."

"I'm going to go back to the hotel, if it's all right with you. It'll be harder for you two to work things out, if I'm hanging around. Unless you need my help with Annalisa. And my vacation is only for a week."

Elyse's eyes widened. "Please don't abandon me."

"I'm not. But you and Luca need this time together—even if it's only related to your daughter. I'm going back to do some sightseeing." She held up a hand. "Don't worry, I'll text you if I run into problems. And if you need a babysitter during the week, I'll be around. After that, you're on your own. And you'll be fine. You all will."

Elyse wasn't so sure about that.

She slung her arm around her aunt's shoulder and squeezed. "I wish I had your certainty, but I do understand." Of course Peggy wouldn't want to be in the room if she and Luca ended up having a huge argument about arrangements. They did need to hammer this out. Without an audience. Even though she hated the thought of being in the house alone with him.

Because of him? Or because she didn't trust herself?

She didn't dare answer that question.

"Thanks for coming with me to Italy. Are you sure you don't want company on your sightseeing tour?"

"I'm positive. I hear there's a romantic gondola tour down the Arno River. Maybe I'll meet a hunky Italian and get lucky."

"Aunt Peggy!"

"Don't you 'Aunt Peggy' me. You're no stranger to the birds and bees or you wouldn't have that sweet little thing in the other room."

She couldn't argue with that.

"You don't even speak Italian."

"Some things you don't need words for. Don't worry. I'll check on you every night until I'm back home in the States."

Elyse smiled. Her aunt was only ten years older than she was, so she was more like a sister than a parental figure. Peggy's husband had been much older than his bride and had died almost five years ago, leaving Peggy a fortune. But it hadn't changed her in the least.

She was still the same fun-loving person she'd always been. She'd even insisted on paying for the trip to Italy.

"Make sure you do. Do I need to set a cur-few?"

Her aunt laughed. "I'd only break it." She kissed her niece on the cheek. "It's not every day I get to see Italy."

Emilia peered around the corner and mo-tioned to them. Judging from the luscious smell coming from the kitchen, breakfast must be ready.

She guessed Anna would be coming with her to the hospital this morning. She smiled. Well, Luca might as well have his first offi-cial reality check about having a baby. He was going to find out it wasn't always convenient. But Elyse wouldn't change it for the world.

Going into the kitchen, she found two plates already set with eggs, ham, thick slices of what looked like homemade toasted bread, and small pots of jam. "This looks delicious. Thank you so much, but aren't you going to eat?"

"Eat...no..." The woman frowned. "Ate six o'clock."

She must have eaten with Luca, then. Glancing at Peg, she said, "Were you here when Luca was eating?"

Peggy sat and dug into her eggs with gusto. "I came after he was done. Emilia offered to make me something then, but I wanted to wait for you."

"I'm sorry. You should have knocked on the door."

"I knew Annalisa would wake you soon enough. I wanted you to get as much sleep as you could."

"Well, I slept great, thank you."

"I'll pack while you're at the hospital so leave the baby with me."

So much for Luca getting his first taste of real fatherhood. "I can take her with me."

"You'll have her to yourself soon enough. I need a few more snuggles before I go, since it looks like I won't be seeing her for a month. That's going to be hard on everyone back home. Especially your mom."

"I know, but it'll fly by."

And if she decided to stay longer than a month?

There was no easy answer. Luca was Anna's father. Nothing was going to change that. And she realized she wouldn't want to, even if she could.

Luca saw her coming down the hall, those hips swinging to an internal tune that he used to know so well. He'd half wondered if she would skip out on him once she found out that Peggy was going back to the hotel.

Her aunt had told him this morning that she wanted to give them time and space to talk things through. He'd tried to insist that she wouldn't be in the way, but she'd turned out to be almost as stubborn as her niece was.

It must run in the family.

Well, it ran in his family too, so he couldn't fault her there.

And he needed to be realistic in his expectations. Elyse had made concessions in coming here, so he needed to make some too. He was going to turn some of his patients over to another neurologist, so he could spend time with his daughter. They could sightsee, or picnic…or whatever the hell Elyse wanted to do. He wasn't courting her, he insisted to himself. He was courting his daughter, hoping to make up for lost time.

At least he hoped that was all it was. Because every time he saw the woman...

He forced that thought back as she reached where he was standing. "Thanks for coming. I have the patient workup waiting in my office. Lorenzo will meet us there in about fifteen minutes to go over everything. Surgery is scheduled for tomorrow."

"I was surprised that you had your own office."

"Yes, didn't you in Atlanta?"

She smiled. "*Touché.* Yes, I did. Sorry."

"It's fine. Anyway, I thought we could discuss the procedure and then see the patient herself. She's American and will probably be happy to see someone from her homeland besides her husband."

"I'm good with that." She sighed. "This is one of those times that I wished I'd paid more attention in Spanish class."

"Spanish?"

"It might help me at least a little bit. I mean, I know I won't need it with this patient, but what if you want me to weigh in on others?"

"Spanish is closer to Portuguese than Italian, although there are some similarities." He smiled. "I can teach you some. I'd really like Annalisa to learn Italian."

Elyse frowned, and he cocked his head. "Is that a problem?"

"No... I just..." The tip of her tongue scrubbed at her upper lip for a second before retreating, but not before the act made something in his gut tighten. He remembered that gesture and a thousand other ones. They were all there in his memory as fresh as the day he'd put them there.

Dio. Would they ever fade?

He hoped not.

Licking her lips normally meant she was going to say something she thought he wouldn't want to hear.

"What is it?"

"My administrator really wants me back at the end of my leave, so I only have this month. Unless I quit my job."

He wanted his parents and sister to meet the baby, but they lived in Rome, almost three hundred kilometers from Florence. They could make the trip there and back by train in a day, but he'd hoped to be able to spend a week or so in Rome to make proper introductions. They still could. It would just have to be carefully arranged.

He needed to call his parents first and let them know they had their first granddaughter. They would be thrilled, even though his folks were a bit old-fashioned about some things.

"We'll figure something out."

"I hope so."

"Is Peggy at the house with Anna?"

"Yes. Did she tell you, she's going back to the hotel and will be returning to Atlanta as planned?"

"Yes. She told me she was going to talk to you about it."

"She did. I'm not sure how I feel about it, but she doesn't want to be in the way. I guess in case we have bitter arguments about Annalisa."

"And will we?"

She looked at him as if needing to consider something. "I really don't want to fight over her. We're both adults, Luca. I'm assuming we both have our daughter's best interests at heart."

Said as if she wasn't sure that he did. That

stung. Made him wonder if she'd ever completely trusted him. With anything. Including her heart.

The end of their relationship said she probably hadn't.

"You assumed correctly. Don't ever doubt it." His answer was sharper than he'd intended it to be and made him realize they were still standing in the middle of the hallway. "Why don't we talk more about Anna after our meeting with Lorenzo?"

"Yes, of course." She looked relieved. "Elevator or stairs?"

"Stairs, if we can. Especially after that huge breakfast Emilia insisted on fixing us."

He smiled. Emilia had worked for his parents for years, helping them throw elaborate parties, so she did tend to go overboard where guests were concerned. Not that he entertained much outside work. He'd never actually brought a woman to the apartment. Hopefully Emilia wouldn't get any funny ideas. "She thinks everything can be solved by a good meal."

If only it were that simple.

They took the stairs to the third floor, where

all of the offices were. Coming out into the main foyer, where leather chairs sat in a large circle on the marble floor, he headed to the far corner, where his office was.

"Why are there so many pictures on the walls? I noticed them downstairs in the entryway as well."

As he saw them every day, they had become so much background noise, but looking at the long line of images he could see how it might look to an outsider. The hospital in Atlanta had been sterile and efficient. But Florence was a city with a rich cultural history as far as art went. "Hospitals have started putting up pictures of nature as a way of enhancing the healing process."

Arched brows went up and she scanned the wall, the bottom half of which was painted blue, whereas a buttery cream covered the upper half. A handrail had been placed along the break in colors, the artwork providing another visual delineation between the two. "Interesting. Do all hospitals in Italy do this?"

"Probably not all of them. It's a relatively new concept. The Clinica Neurologica di Firenze adopted it about five years ago."

"Firenze?"

It was easy to forget, even with all the tourists, that the name of the hospital meant nothing to a non-Italian speaker. "Sorry, it's the way we say Florence."

He smiled, remembering the way she would puzzle through an Italian phrase, trying to make sense of it, when they had been together. She'd loved him speaking Italian while they made love, the little sounds she'd made sending him spinning into space more than once. Long before he'd been ready.

He swallowed. Not something he wanted to remember.

Unlocking his office, he motioned her inside. "What time do you need to get back to relieve Peggy?"

"I think I have a few hours. I'm still nursing, but more in the morning and at night, since I was getting ready to go back to work. I've been supplementing with bottles for the last couple of weeks."

"Okay, sounds good."

There was a knock on the door and Lorenzo opened the door a crack and said, "C'è stato um cambiamento di piani."

Luca motioned him inside, answering him in English. "A change of plans? What kind of change?" He inserted, "Sorry. Lorenzo, you remember Elyse?"

"Yes. Of course." He took her hand and smiled at her. "But you must call me Enzo." Her cheeks flushed a deep red. "Okay."

What the hell? Luca's eyes narrowed, centering squarely on his friend. "You mentioned that something had changed."

"Yes, Mary Landers has had two seizures in the last two hours. I've moved surgery up from tomorrow to today. In two hours, to be exact. I have to prepare in a few minutes, but I would like to run by you the method I'm planning on using, Elyse, if you don't mind."

"Of course not. Can we go over the chart together?"

Luca pulled the chart he had and handed it to Lorenzo. Soon the pair were going over things, heads bent close as they studied and discussed the findings. He didn't like the way they looked together, her blond locks contrasting with Lorenzo's close-cut black hair. Elyse spoke in quick, concise statements, explaining her case and how it was similar to and different from the one at hand. "My patient didn't have back-to-back seizures like this one, but they're similar. And going in with a ventriculoscopy followed by microsurgery is the same method I would choose if she were my patient."

Lorenzo looked at her and said, "Perfect. *Grazie.* Will you be observing?"

"If possible."

"Yes. There's a microphone in the observation room. If something strikes you during the surgery, feel free to mention it. Also, it might help the patient if you went in and spoke with her beforehand."

"I will. Thanks."

He took her hand again and gave it a squeeze. "See you soon."

Luca frowned. What was with his friend? And since when did he ask anyone to call him Enzo?

But before he could even formulate a response, Lorenzo was out the door.

"Are you sure you have time to observe? It will probably last several hours."

"Peggy has enough supplies for quite a while. I'll give her a quick call though and check." She glanced at him. "Are you scrubbing in as well?"

"They have another neurophysiologist who will be monitoring the patient's readings, but I'll be available to interpret a scan if they need it during the ventriculoscopy."

He remembered the first time he'd heard mention of a burr hole and realized that drilling through the skull was a practice that hadn't entirely faded out with time. It still had its place, and this was one of them.

"I wish embolization techniques worked for these types of malformations, but they don't."

He'd always liked talking about work with her. She was intelligent and thoughtful. Not hurried, not intimidated, even though neurology was still a male-dominated field. She wasn't in it to show anyone up. But she wasn't afraid to push back over a diagnosis either, which he'd witnessed firsthand. The death of a patient had changed things between them. She'd stopped discussing cases with him, had become distant and moody. It had continued until the layoff occurred.

He'd never been able to figure out exactly what had happened between them.

no idea what, because the only thing he could think of doing right now was kissing her.

Unless…that's exactly what she was waiting for.

That was enough for him.

His hands went to her shoulders and he stood there for several long seconds.

Then he kissed her.

"No, it would be wonderful if it was a relatively easy fix, but with the type of procedure Lorenzo is going to do, he'll have to enlarge the burr hole to double its size and go in manually."

"Hopefully the seizures are caused by the cavernoma and not something else," she said.

"Testing has pretty much ruled out anything else." He paused. "Are you ready to go see her?"

"Yes. And thank you for asking me to come."

"You're welcome."

He put the computer to sleep and they both stood, trying to exit the same side of the desk. They bumped shoulders and she gave a husky

CHAPTER FIVE

THE SECOND HIS lips touched hers, her eyes slammed shut, and she was trapped in a warm sea of familiarity. One she'd blocked from her thoughts until this very moment. His mouth was firm, just like it had been, his taste exactly the same: dark roasted coffee and everything that went along with being Luca.

"*Dio.*" He came up long enough to mutter that single oath before kissing her again.

The word made her whole body liquefy. She could remember long strings of Italian that would help drive her to the very brink of ecstasy, and then hold her there until he was ready to send her over the edge. And then he would start all over. A slow, wonderful torture that she never wanted to end.

Her arms went around his neck, and she pressed herself against him, needing to get closer even as he edged her back until her

bottom was against the back of the chair. She struggled to balance herself on it, even as she wanted to turn and lean over it, inviting an exploration of a different type.

Lord, she was in trouble. Big trouble, but she didn't want to stop. Didn't want to do anything that would change the course of where this might be headed.

She'd missed him so very much.

His hand went to her breast, palm pressing against her tight nipple with a caress that sent a shock wave through her. And something else.

A warning tingle. Oh, no!

It was the signal that her body had felt the stimulation and completely mistaken the reason for it.

Her hands went to his shoulders and pushed, terrified she would end up with two wet circles on the front of her blue blouse.

As soon as his mouth came off hers, and he took a step back, she crossed her arms over her chest and applied pressure, hoping it didn't look as obvious as it felt. It worked. The tide began to recede.

In the meantime, Luca dragged a hand

through his hair that she could swear shook a little. "*Dio*, Elyse. Sorry. I didn't call you to my office for that." His accent was suddenly thicker than normal.

She knew he hadn't. If he'd been interested in sex, there was always the house.

A house they would now be spending a lot of time in...largely alone.

She almost groaned aloud. If something like this happened when they accidentally bumped into each other, what would happen when it wasn't an accident?

Ha! She wasn't about to find out. She would have to keep their daughter between them as much as possible. Surely he wouldn't kiss her while she was holding Anna.

If she was embarrassed now, what would she be like if there were no clothes, no way to hide what was happening?

It was a natural process. Nothing to be ashamed of. She used her breasts to nourish her baby.

But they were also sexual. And right now it was hard to separate one from the other. She wasn't sure she even wanted to. She'd just assumed she wouldn't have sex again until after

Anna was weaned, since there were no prospects hovering on the horizon. Not even a blip on the radar.

The breakup between her and Luca had been too traumatic. And with the shared reality of a baby, it was still too raw. Anna connected Luca to her in a very tangible way. That connection was now permanent, like it or not.

He was looking at her, waiting for some kind of response to his apology.

"It was both of us, not just you. I think our emotions—you finding out you have a child and me finding out that you want to be a part of her life—got the better of us."

Did she really believe that? Not for one second. It had been the past coming back to haunt her that had caused it.

"Yes, that must be it." The words were half muttered as if he hadn't really meant her to hear them.

He was staring at her chest, and she really arms were still tightly crossed over it. tingling had stopped she could of She unfolded them and ides. There was no hy she'd been doing that, but hopefully he hadn't seen it as a self-protective gesture. It had been, but not in the way he might think.

She smiled. "Florence is a very romantic city. I'll have to watch my step from here on out."

"No. No, you won't."

The way he said it gave her pause. Was he saying he wasn't going to have a problem staying away from her? Well, that was good. Wasn't it?

Yes, it was. "Well, now that we've settled that, shall we actually go see the patient? Preferably before they prep her for surgery? I'd like to see how she is."

"Of course. The surgical unit is on the first floor, so it's back down the stairs for us. Or would you rather—?"

"The stairs are fine." She needed to keep moving. At least for now. The hope was that it would keep her from thinking too much

A few minutes later, they were i Landers's room, and she chatted English. The woman seem another native spe husband, and

Maybe it was just knowing that Elyse was in the medical profession that made her feel more at ease. "The procedure should help you feel a lot better."

"Will it clear up my double vision?"

"That's the hope. As well as the seizures and your other problems." She glanced back at Luca for confirmation.

He inclined his head. "You might not notice a huge difference right away, but once the inflammation from the malformation is gone, things should settle down."

"I hope so. Todd wanted me to go back to the States to have the procedure, but I just wanted to get it over with. And we read that this center is one of the best in Europe." She reached for her husband's hand.

"We do quite a few procedures on blood vessel problems. Cavernomas are fairly rare but, even so, they're well studied."

A nurse came in. "It is almost time. Are you ready?" Her English wasn't quite as fluent as some of the others', but it was enough to elicit a smile from their patient.

"More than ready." She squeezed her husband's hand and he leaned down to kiss her on the forehead.

"Love you."

"You'll be here when I get out?"

"I'm not going anywhere, sweetheart. Ever."

The words brought a lump to Elyse's throat. She resisted the urge to look over her shoulder to see what Luca's expression was—or if there was even any reaction at all.

Would he have been like this in the delivery room as she'd had Anna?

It was too late now. She'd never know. The lump turned to an ache that wouldn't go away. Mary was wheeled from the room and Todd followed her, giving them a nod of his head. She forced herself to speak. "Do we need to help him find the waiting room?"

"One of the nurses will show him where to go. He can walk with Mary as far as the doors of the surgical suite. It's kind of a ritual. Most loved ones accompany their family members."

"I don't blame them. I would too." She'd had no one but her mom and dad when they'd had to do the C-section for Annalisa. Luca had been long gone.

Not a helpful thought.

She was curious, though. "Did you come to Florence as soon as you left the States?"

She wasn't sure why she asked that, but once the words were out, there was no way to retract them.

"No, I spent some time in Rome with my folks first." He motioned for her to walk down a corridor. "By the way, I would like them to meet Annalisa, if you'd be willing."

That caught her up short for a second or two. She hadn't even thought about that.

"Yes. Of course. I can't imagine there *not* being time, even if I'm only here for a month."

They came to a set of double doors with red lettering that she took to mean authorized personnel only beyond that point. "Do I need a visitor's pass or anything?"

"As long as you're with me, you'll be fine." Would she? She could remember a time when that hadn't been the case, when being with him had been anything but fine. That had been right before he'd left for parts unknown, and she'd never seen him again.

Until now.

She swallowed. He wanted his parents to

meet Annalisa. Of course he did. She was their granddaughter. "How far is Rome?"

"It's about an hour and a half by train. Double that by car."

She remembered his patient load. "You'll be able to get time off work?"

"I should be able to move things around."

Luca led the way to a set of doors each with a number and the words "Sala Operatoria." Operating Suite, maybe? It was amazing how she could kind of decipher certain terms. But that was only if she was standing there studying them. Hearing someone speak was an entirely different matter. Even the word for Florence sounded nothing like the English word. It looked like the word for fire or something.

"In here."

He motioned to a room marked "Sala di Osservazione."

She went through and saw a tiered bank of about fifteen seats. There were already three people in there on the far side of the room chatting in low voices. Judging by their white lab coats, she assumed they were either still in medical school or were first-year residents. It didn't look like an entire class, since none of them had that "professor" look to them.

There was also a microphone hanging front and center, just as Enzo had told her there would be.

Luca found them seats in the front row toward the middle, and she sat, looking at the room below with interest. "Will they pipe sound in here? I know Enzo said we could make comments."

"Yes, *Enzo* did."

Why had he emphasized his colleague's name like that?

Before she could attempt to figure it out, he went on, "There's a microphone hanging above the operating table, just like in the States, and everything in the room is recorded. Surgeons are encouraged to relay what they are doing. All of it will go on record, unless there's an emergency, then everyone focuses on the patient's welfare above all else."

She had turned her head toward him to focus on what he was saying, only she kept finding her gaze dropping to the movement of his lips. Lips that had been on hers a few moments earlier. Not good. That kiss had done a number on her. She needed to forget it. Chalk it up to the rekindling of old emotions.

Only she'd thought those were all dead.

She jerked her attention back to the front, hoping he hadn't noticed. Maybe it was the lack of closure that was messing with her equilibrium. There'd been no time for closure. She'd received word that his job as well as several others were being done away with. She'd announced the news. They'd had frantic sex. And he'd left. Just like that. It had been a whirlwind breakup.

Nothing clean about it.

Her thoughts were interrupted when they wheeled the patient into the room. Enzo entered already scrubbed and ready and was bent over the patient.

"He's talking to her about what's going to happen. He likes to look his patients in the eye before beginning and asking if they have any questions."

"That's a little different than how I do it, but I like it." Elyse normally didn't come in until the patient was already sedated and surgery was ready to begin. But she did stay with them until they came out from under anesthesia and also visited them in Recovery—when they were more likely to remember her.

The surgeon then moved away, and his team gathered around him, except for one of the nurses and the anesthesiologist, who began administering the sedation drugs.

"It looks kind of like a football huddle."

"That is basically what it is. They're getting any last-minute information, and Lorenzo is making sure they know which instruments he plans to use and the order he'll need them." He glanced at her. "They're surgical nurses so they tend to be intuitive, and most of them know what to expect, but it still helps to be reminded."

Yes, it did. Just like she'd reminded herself a few minutes ago that their relationship wasn't just under general anesthesia. It had flatlined and was gone, not surviving what life had thrown at it. She shouldn't go looking for it to wake up and recover, like Mrs. Landers would hopefully do.

the patient was sedated, and the area where the surgery would take shaved and had a sterile

"He'll do the trepanning first." It's what they had talked about. It would result in the burr hole being drilled to a larger diameter, but the smaller hole gave the endoscope a solid surface on which to rest as it was guided through the delicate tissue.

"Yes. He'll want a precise location and size before actually going in to remove it," Luca replied.

Even though there would be a record of those things on the MRI scans, nothing replaced having a physical look at it.

"I'm surprised you're not down there in the mix." She looked over at the monitor and saw a man to the left of the patient, checking the tracings. A neurophysiologist. Just like Luca. He would be monitoring the patient's brain function during surgery.

"It was a last-minute change in plans, remember? The surgery was supposed to be tomorrow. I told him I'd be available for a second opinion, if needed."

"You were supposed to be in the o̶p̶e̶r̶a̶t̶i̶n̶g̶ room tomorrow? What happen̶e̶d̶ ̶t̶o̶ ̶g̶e̶t̶ you in there now?"

He looked at h̶

happened. Anna happened. I need to free up my time. I'll be doing more of that in the coming weeks."

She swallowed then laid her hand on his arm, squeezing lightly. "I'm so sorry, Luca. Our coming here has totally disrupted your life."

"Not disrupted. I would call it more... *deviare*."

Anna had disrupted hers as well, but she wouldn't trade it for the world.

Her head cocked to the side, trying to figure out what the word meant. Devi...something. Deviate, maybe? From what?

"I think the word in English is to re-road?"

"Ah, reroute?" Okay, that was much better than deviated. Because to deviate from one's planned path was...

Exactly what she'd done. But it wasn't horrible. She'd adapted, and she was happy. Happier than she'd ever been, in fact. The only part that made her truly sad was knowing she couldn't have any more children like her daughter.

"Yes, reroute. But I am glad you came. Glad you told me the truth."

Even though she was more than four months late. More than that, if you counted the pregnancy itself. And she hadn't told him the entire truth, but the rest of her story didn't matter. It didn't affect him. Just her.

She glanced down when the sound of the cranial drill engaged. She remembered practicing how to stop precisely when the skull wall was breached so as not to damage the grey matter below. Newer technology was arriving and there were now drills that came with measured stops that took some of the thinking out of it.

Within seconds, they'd reached their goal, the hole swabbed, and the endoscope fed through. A screen on the far wall went live—she was pretty sure that was for the benefit of those in the observation room. Enzo looked through the overhead surgical microscope as the tube made its way toward the ventricle in question. With each step, he relayed to the listening device what he was doing and what he saw, with Luca translating close to her ear so as not to disturb the others in the room.

The tickle of his warm breath hitting her

skin was intimate. Almost unbearably so. But she didn't want him to stop. In fact, she propped her chin on the back of her hand and let herself enjoy listening to the sound of his voice.

"Approaching lateral ventricle. Entering space." There was a pause while Enzo readjusted his instruments and probably took stock of what was appearing on the screen. "Malformation is approximately three centimeters in diameter, causing a slight deformity of the left side."

The voice in her ear stopped when the voice on the loudspeaker halted, but the reactions happening inside her head kept right on going, setting up a weird tingle that made her shiver. She'd told herself to enjoy it, but she was starting to like it a little too much.

There was a period of silence that went on for about thirty seconds. It was almost as if the room had gone into a state of suspended animation, with everyone waiting for Dr. Giorgino's verdict.

As much as she wanted Luca to continue, maybe she'd be better off wishing the surgery ended quickly. Before she did something stupid. Like she had during that kiss.

Enzo lifted his head and spoke. And so did Luca.

"We should be able to dissect it with minimal damage."

The words made her swallow, but it engendered a very different reaction from others in the room. Muscles that were tense went slack with relief.

The surgeon then called out orders as the burr hole was enlarged enough for the instruments he would use. She understood none of it.

"Do you want me to keep translating?"

"If something important happens, I'd like to know, but I'm familiar enough with the surgery to understand what's happening on the screen. Thank you, though. I did want to know what his verdict was."

She forced a smile, telling herself she was relieved that his lips were no longer at her ear. But there was also a sense of loss that she was no longer allowed those kinds of privileges.

He sat back in his chair, and Elyse thought she saw a hint of relief in his own eyes. Maybe she wasn't the only one affected by their proximity.

They'd been very good together in bed. He had taken her places she'd never been before. Her relationship with Kyle had paled beside him. She somehow doubted anyone else would move her the way Luca had, even though their time together hadn't been all that long. Just four months.

She'd never met his parents, although he'd met hers. Then again, her parents lived within an hour's drive of the hospital, while his lived on a different continent.

And yet he wanted them to meet Annalisa. He'd never said whether or not he'd told them about living with her in the States. She'd never asked, because she'd thought they had plenty of time for all of that.

Only they hadn't.

Elyse forced herself to settle in to watch the rest of the procedure, noting the similarities and differences between what was done in this center compared to what she would have done back home. She made a mental note to herself to research a couple of items to see if anyone was using the techniques she was seeing here. Maybe she could learn a thing or two.

Had Luca carried any techniques back from the States with him? She was curious.

"Did you change the way you do things at all after you came back? Or is neurophysiology basically the same here as it is in Atlanta?"

"Why do you ask?" The look on his face was of genuine puzzlement.

"I don't know. I'm just curious. I've seen a couple of things that I'm going to look into. The order in which Enzo clamped off those blood vessels is a little different. Not in a bad way. I liked what I saw on the screen."

"Ahh, I see. Yes, I think there are things that I probably changed. Things I learned or saw during my time at your hospital that I have applied here."

Your hospital. A sting of pain went through her.

It had been his at one time too. Until she'd severed his connection to it.

Actually, she hadn't severed it. The administration had, and there'd been nothing she could do about it.

You could have quit too. It might have saved your relationship with Luca.

Doubtful. He'd asked her if she had put his name on the list of people to be fired. She hadn't. But at the time she'd been glad it was there, thinking that if she was no longer his boss, maybe some of her conflicted emotions about dating someone she worked so closely with would dissipate. Her reaction had probably been a knee-jerk one, and not entirely rational, but it had been very real. To her, anyway.

He was extremely talented, she'd thought. He could have worked anywhere in Atlanta. He hadn't wanted to do that, though. Neither had he seemed interested in salvaging what they'd had.

How much of that had been her doing? Probably a lot. And she owed him an apology.

Keeping her voice low, she said, "Luca, I'm sorry for the way things at the hospital unfolded. I know it wasn't easy. For any of you."

She hesitated, but needed to get the rest of it out. "I didn't put your name on that list. I had no idea who was on it until it was handed to me. But I should have found a way to warn you before I told everyone else. At the time, though, I was worried about that being seen as playing favorites."

"Playing favorites. We were living together at the time, no?" His jaw tightened. "It doesn't matter. It's…how do you say it? Water under the bridge. It's over."

Yes, it was. And so were they. The anguish of that day still washed over her at times. Except now they had a baby. Someone who could make her smile, make her glad that that period of her life had happened, despite the way it had ended.

Needing to pull herself together, she took her phone out of her pocket and checked it for text messages. There were none. Peggy knew her well enough to call or text if anything happened, even if it wasn't a big deal.

"Everything okay?" he murmured.

"Yes, just making sure Peggy wasn't trying to get a hold of me for anything."

"What time do you want to get home?"

The words confused her for a second, then she realized he was talking about his house, not her place back in Atlanta. "If the surgery won't run too long, I'm fine staying until the end."

They were still speaking in hushed tones, but Luca hadn't tried to lean in close to her again, for which she was thankful.

Ears were now off-limits.

Although she wasn't sure how she was going to break that to him if he decided to translate for her again, or if she even wanted him to.

Because she had a strange feeling that if he leaned in and started whispering again, she would sit there and pay rapt attention. Not to the words. But to the way he made her feel.

Not good, Elyse.

But how exactly was she going to stop her reaction? It was almost as elemental as the tingling in her breasts had been during that kiss.

The man coaxed feelings from her that she neither wanted nor needed.

No, scratch that. She didn't need them, but she did want them.

Wanted them enough to kiss him, as she'd already proved.

So how was she going to fix that and prevent it from happening again?

Simple, she needed to avoid situations where her self-control was at risk.

Ha! You mean something like living under the same roof as the man? A stone's throw from his bedroom?

She sighed. Yes. Exactly like that.

Only now that she'd gotten herself into that situation, she had no idea how to get herself back out of it.

CHAPTER SIX

ANNA CHORTLED WHEN Luca bit into his toast. He cocked his head, trying to figure out what was so funny about it.

"She laughs at odd things. It's like she's trying to figure out her world."

Elyse had evidently noted his confusion and tried to explain what was behind it.

Watching the baby on her lap, he forked up a bite of egg, giving an exaggerated *"mmm..."* of pleasure, and the laugh got louder, turned infectious enough that Elyse started giggling along with her.

"Who knew eating could be so amusing?"

"She's only doing it to you."

To prove her point, Elyse picked up her toast and bit off a piece of it, chewing with exaggerated movements of her jaw. Anna didn't even spare her mom a glance. She just kept staring at Luca.

He tapped his finger on the very end of the baby's nose. "Glad you find your...father...so funny."

Why had he hesitated over saying that? Was it because he still didn't quite believe a child so perfect and beautiful could possibly be his? Elyse had already offered to have a DNA test done but, like he'd told her, he didn't need one. The baby was his. He felt it in his bones. There were things about her coloring, how different her hair was from her mother's, that made him sure that Annalisa was from his family.

Except for the dimple in the baby's cheek, which she definitely got from her *mamma*. Elyse had a dimple on the very same side of her face. He could remember touching it when she smiled, fascinated by the way it puckered inward. It was hellishly attractive. And when he saw Elyse in his dreams, she always had that secret dimple.

He dreamed about her.

He could finally admit it to himself, if not to her. But he hadn't quite figured out how to deal with those dreams. And when he had been translating for Lorenzo a couple of days ago, it had come back to him that he'd muttered in her ear in one such dream, saying all the things he wanted to do to her. He'd woken up hard, needing her so badly. Only she hadn't been there. It had all been in his head.

Well, not all of it. It had been elsewhere too. When his body had begun to react to those memories as he'd translated for the surgeon, he'd decided he needed to stop it. He'd backed off, needing to get himself under control. He'd thanked his lucky stars when she'd told him she didn't need him to translate for her anymore.

"I called my parents yesterday."

She stopped playing with Anna's fingers. "You did? What did they say?"

There was a nervousness to her voice that he didn't like. "I didn't exactly tell them. Not yet. I thought maybe it would be better just to let them see her and then explain it."

"I don't know… It was easier with my parents. Although they were upset that you'd left, I told them it was my fault, but they didn't quite believe me, I don't think."

"I was hurt. And angry. And things hadn't been going well between us for a while. I thought this was maybe your way of pushing me out of the picture."

She frowned. "I would have told you, if that were the case."

"So you think things were actually good?"

"I didn't say that."

He set down his fork. "You don't have to. We were over before you ever read out that list of names, and you know it."

"I guess we were."

She didn't look happy about that. Then again, she hadn't looked happy at the time either. She'd just looked…guilty.

He'd caught that same expression on her face a couple of times since she'd arrived in Italy, but he wasn't sure what that was about. At first he'd thought it was about her possible involvement in getting him fired. But she'd already made her big confession about that. And yet even this morning she'd glanced at him and then looked away quickly.

Was she hiding something? Something other than her part in the layoffs?

He couldn't imagine what it might be. Or how it would even have anything to do with him, at this point. If Anna was his, that was the only thing that was important.

"You're okay with Mamma and Papà meeting her? And you, of course."

"I guess so. It's bound to be a shock, though. What if they hate me? I had convinced myself that because you didn't want children, you wouldn't want her either. I decided I'd come, do what I thought was right and then turn around and go home. I didn't stop to think who else might be impacted by the delay."

"I love her. How could I not? What I said back then about not wanting kids was...a moment of stupidity." She wasn't the only one who hadn't stopped to think about the impact of his behavior—or his words. He could see why she'd been afraid to tell him about Anna. "I'll just accentuate the positives when I tell them."

Her brows went up, and she shifted Anna to the other side of her lap. "Which are?"

"The fact that they have a healthy, happy grandchild. And..." What were the positives other than that? It was hard to list them when she said it in that tone of voice. "And they will fall in love with Anna as soon as they meet her."

"I hope so." She took another bite of her toast, chewing for a long time.

She was worried. So was he, for that matter. But what he'd said was true. Once they got over their surprise, they would welcome both Elyse and Annalisa with open arms. His mom would probably even try her hand at matchmaking—which he needed to shoot down right away and firmly explain that he and Elyse were no longer together, neither would they change their minds.

Was he so sure about that? He'd been positive that Elyse would forever reject his requests for a date. Then one day—out of the blue—she'd taken his hand and asked him instead. But that didn't mean she was suddenly going turn the tables and ask him to marry her.

If she'd accepted his proposal, would they be making an engagement announcement to his parents instead of just a birth announcement?

But she hadn't. And they weren't.

"It will be fine." He wasn't sure if he was

trying to convince himself or her. "How is Peggy doing?"

Elyse smiled. "She's doing great, from what her texts and social media accounts say. She is taking full advantage of her newfound freedom. She's even been out on a date, which I did not approve of, by the way."

"You don't want her falling for an Italian?"

She laughed. "Since I fell for one once, that's not the issue. It's the fact that she's not going to be here long enough to start up anything meaningful."

"And encounters must always be meaningful?" He wondered if she would remember the first time they'd slept together. He had waited for that first date for so very long and when it had happened...it had been impulsive and wild, and she'd hooked him from the moment he'd caught his breath.

She looked away, those cheeks of hers turning a shade of pink that made his insides shift.

She did remember.

"At least we were living in the same country at the time," she said.

"So you wouldn't have given me the time of day if I'd been a tourist in your country?"

She wrinkled her nose at him. "Probably not. And since I was department head, I really shouldn't have done so even then." Her face went serious. "Those dynamics are never a good idea. I think we proved that."

He touched Annalisa's hand, the thought bothering him somehow. "And yet if we hadn't gotten together, Annalisa wouldn't exist. Wasn't she worth it?"

Her teeth came down on her lip. There was a pause. One that was long enough to turn uncomfortable. Then she said huskily, "Yes. She was worth it. I'd do it all over again, even knowing what I know now."

"So would I."

She gave a sigh. "Hopefully your parents will feel the same way. That having a grandchild is okay even without having daughter-in-law attached. Someday, I'm sure you'll meet a wonderful Italian girl and settle down. Maybe you'll even change your mind about wanting kids sooner rather than later."

"I think I already have. Quite some time ago, actually. Things just didn't work out quite the way I thought they would."

"You did? I—I didn't realize."

Why had she said it that way? Was she hoping he already had someone so that she was free to pursue whoever she wanted? Would she get married and allow his daughter to become someone else's?

"I already have a child. Don't ever forget that."

She caught his hand. "I didn't mean it like that, Luca. I just meant that Annalisa isn't the only grandchild they're likely to have. And you're probably not going to be single the rest of your life."

He didn't see himself getting involved with anyone else for the foreseeable future, and he wasn't sure why. He'd immersed himself in work for so long, he wasn't sure he knew how to stop. At least he'd thought that until Elyse had come back into his life. And now suddenly he was rearranging everything in his life for her.

No, not everything. And it was for Anna, not for Elyse.

Only the hand holding his said that wasn't entirely true.

"For now, I'll leave it to my sisters to give

them grandchildren. If they ever meet some-one, that is."

He hadn't thought about what might happen if Elyse met someone else and they had a baby together. Would her husband or boyfriend in-sist she cut off contact with him? Deny him access to Anna?

That thought made him feel physically ill. "I know we talked about it before, but I'd still like to draw up an agreement."

As soon as he saw her face, he realized it was the wrong thing to say. She let go of him and drew Annalisa closer to her. "What kind of agreement?"

He could have said a custody agreement, but he knew that would be met with swift re-sistance. Besides, she'd come to Italy in good faith, trying to do the right thing. She'd said so herself. And if he thought about it, Elyse was not the type of person to let herself be railroaded into anything.

He chose his words carefully. "About visi-tation."

The wariness didn't fade from her eyes. If anything, it grew. "You think we need something formal in writing? I wasn't planning on keeping her from you."

His intent hadn't been to make her angry, but something was going on with her that he really didn't understand.

"You talked about me meeting someone else, and it made me think about the reverse. That you might meet someone who wouldn't want me involved in your life or Annalisa's."

Her grip on the baby loosened. "Would *you* do that, if you had a child and started dating someone else: prevent the other parent from seeing him or her?"

"No. I wouldn't." There was no hesitation in his answer because it was the truth.

"Well, I wouldn't let someone do that to you either, Luca. I would never keep her from you unless I thought it was for her own good."

Her own good? How would that ever be the case?

It wouldn't. So stop being so sensitive to every little thing.

That was going to be hard. Because, like it or not, Elyse was only here for a little while. A month was nothing, in the greater scheme of things. And where Elyse went, Annalisa went.

"When you say 'for her own good' I'm not sure what that means."

She raised her brows and then grinned. "Well, let's see… If you were in an Italian prison on a life sentence for murder, I might hesitate before bringing her to see you."

He laughed. "Since I don't see that happening, I would have to have been wrongly convicted."

He'd been trying to lighten the mood, just like she had, but it must have fallen short because her smile faded. "What if you married someone who was unkind to Anna?"

Another hint that she had no intention of getting back together with him? It shouldn't sting, but it did.

"I will make sure that never happens." Not only because there were no current prospects but because he would never do anything to harm his daughter.

"How can you be so sure? Sometimes people aren't exactly who they seem on the surface."

He leaned closer, making sure she heard every word he said. "You seem determined to set me up with some unknown—but evidently unhinged—person. Why is that?"

"What? I'm not. I'm just setting up a hypothetical situation."

"Let's turn it around. What if you date a series of commitment-phobes and make Anna think relationships never last?" Lorenzo's knowing smile popped into his head. That man wouldn't know a serious relationship if it bit him on the ass. What if Elyse decided she liked that kind of man? After all, she seemed to have moved on with her life without a backward glance at him.

"I wouldn't. I won't. But I understand what you're saying. Let's just agree that we'll both try to do whatever's in her best interests."

The tense muscles along his shoulders eased ... ir grip. "Agreed. Speaking of things that ... nalisa's best interests, we've already ... oing to see my parents. Would ... it being in the next cou- ... short notice, but I've ... nd I think I can ... ith them."

"No, I think I just expected us to have time to figure things out before jumping in at the deep end."

"If we wait until we iron out every tiny detail, Anna will be eighteen."

He'd decided that waiting for a break in his schedule wasn't going to happen if he didn't make it happen. This was the first step in doing that.

"You're right, of course. Let me check with Peggy, so she doesn't think I just abandoned her."

He'd forgotten about her aunt. "Does she need you to stay close by?"

"Are you kidding? She's pretty independent. I just meant that if she got into some kind of difficult situation, I'd want her to know how to reach me and that I'd be a few hours aw

Oh! What should I take for a gift?"

"For my parents? No need to

thing."

Annalisa started

from her tiny

thing. I kn

they?"

"Annalisa will be the only gift they need. They'll be thrilled to meet her and spend some time with her."

"I'm going to be stubborn on this one. Can you point me in the direction of a store that might have something they would like?"

He sighed. She wasn't going to take no for an answer. "Here in Italy flowers and wine are traditional gifts for a hostess, although I hope you'll think of my mother as more than just a hostess. She's Annalisa's grandmother."

"I know that. Really, I do. Any particular type of flowers?"

"Just not carnations. I know you use a lot of those in the States, but here they are primarily used for mourning and funerals."

"Okay." Her eyes widened. "Thanks for telling me that, because I almost certainly would have brought the wrong thing."

"I'll leave a couple of hours early on Friday and we can get something before boarding the train. There are shops not far from the station."

Annalisa wiggled and gave another—angrier sounding—cry. At which point Luca smelled something that wasn't quite right. In fact, it smelled a little bit like...

Poop.

No wonder she was fussy.

"Do you have a diaper bag nearby?"

"Why?" She glanced at the baby and then up at him. "Oh...she..."

"I do believe she's filled her diaper."

"I'll take her." She stood and reached her arms out for the baby, waiting until she was back in her possession before continuing. "I need to feed her, anyway, so I might as well change her too. We can go over Diapering for Beginners at another time."

He smiled, liking the fact that she was willing to let him take on some of Anna's care. Elyse had talked about her aunt being independent. Well, it must be a family trait, because that independent streak reached to the furthest branches on that particular family tree. "I'll look forward to it."

"Hmm." She rocked the baby back and forth.

"Wait until you have one that shoots halfway up her back. You may change your mind."

"I won't. I promise." He nodded at his phone,

which was on the counter. "I'll get the dishes cleaned up and then go to the hospital for a couple of hours. Maybe afterward we can do a little bit of sightseeing in town, if you and Anna are up for it."

"We will be, if you're sure you have the time."

"I'm learning to make time for what's important."

The smile she gave him reached her eyes, crinkling them at the corners. "Thank you, Luca. For everything."

She showed him how to strap the baby into the car seat she'd brought, unexpectedly nervous about spending time with him. Which was ridiculous. She'd spent loads of time with him when he'd lived in Atlanta. But this was different. That had been on her turf. And now she wasn't. She also had Annalisa to worry about as well. What if the baby was so fussy that she got on his nerves?

No, Luca was one of the most patient men she'd ever known. The only time she'd seen him truly irritated was when an insurance agency had tried to tell him that the procedure he'd wanted to do on a patient was experimental and wouldn't be covered. He'd hit the roof, going to the hospital administrator and demanding he help the company change their minds. Instead, the administrator had needed to sit Luca down and explain the way things worked in their health care system.

After a series of appeals and a peer-to-peer call between the insurance agency's doctor and Luca, they'd gotten it ironed out and the patient had gotten the surgery, which had ended up saving her life. From then on he'd been firm and insistent, but had followed the rules. In fact, Luca had been able to finagle more insurance coverage for patients than her, and she always tried her hardest.

It was in his voice. That deep mellow baritone that still made her knees go weak. It worked its magic on everyone. Except for hospital bean counters who were only worried about the profit margins and sometimes didn't see the faces behind their decisions. Like when they downsized her department. Now she was seriously overworked. So was everyone who was left in Neurology. In fact, Elyse wasn't taking new patients at all. She didn't have the time.

"There—is that right?" He fiddled with the straps to the car seat even after she'd assured him it was perfect.

"You're a careful driver, Luca, which helps."

He said maybe he'd changed his mind about having kids. When had that happened? When he'd seen his daughter for the first time? Her eyes closed, a lump forming in her throat. She was glad that he might want more. Wasn't she?

Thank God she hadn't accepted his marriage proposal only to find out he did indeed want more children.

He leaned over and kissed Annalisa's forehead, turning the lump in Elyse's throat into a boulder. "I will be even more careful than usual."

They got in, and he waited for her to buckle in as well. She gave an inward eye roll, swallowing down her earlier emotions and moving to a neutral subject. "How is Mrs. Landers?"

"I checked in on her yesterday. She's recovering nicely. They're hoping she can go home in a few more days. They want to make sure there's no more seizure activity first."

"Will they do physical therapy with her to help strengthen some of the affected muscles?"

"Yes, there is a rehab facility right next to the neural science clinic. And she'll be followed up by Lorenzo for a couple of months. Any scans will come through me, so I'll be able to see how she's doing as well."

In a couple of months Elyse would be long gone. She wasn't sure how she felt about that anymore.

Then they were on their way into the center of the city, where the famous Florence Cathedral could be seen.

"Why do you call the cathedral the *Duomo?*"

"It means dome, which is why most of the residents just use that, rather than its formal name, which is Cattedrale di Santa Maria del Fiore."

"Wow that's a mouthful. I can see how the Dome would be easier." Not only was it a mouthful but hearing Luca speak his native tongue still turned her insides to mush.

How was that even possible?

Within fifteen minutes they had found a paid parking area for the car. "Most of these are done with tour guides. We can join one of the groups, or we can do our own thing, whichever you prefer."

"I'm sure you know just about as much as the guides, so could we do it on our own, just in case Annalisa decides to give us trouble." She got out of the car and unstrapped the baby from the seat.

"I'll carry her."

"Are you sure? She gets heavy pretty quickly. I have a sling."

"She's as light as a feather. And, yes, I'm sure. Just show me how to put it on."

She helped Luca get fitted with the sling, surprised he would let himself be seen with something like that. But she had to admit he looked beyond sexy whenever he held Anna. Women were going to envy her. Little did they know they had nothing to fear.

He was available. But not today. Her chin went up. Today he was all hers.

She snuggled Anna into the curve of the carrier. The poor thing blinked up at them as if trying to figure out what kind of trick this was.

It wasn't a trick, and Elyse had to admit she felt a trickle of jealousy. She used to love lying against the man's chest when they were in bed. And now they had a baby.

Before she could stop herself, she took her phone and snapped a picture of him.

"What are you doing?"

She had no idea. Just knew she wanted something to remember this moment by when she got back to the States. "She'll want pictures of you together."

It was a lie, but there was no way she was going to tell him the true reason. That there was something heartbreakingly beautiful about seeing him and Anna together.

He smiled. "As long as you don't plan to use it as blackmail material."

"Ha! No."

He settled the baby a little closer to his midsection, curving his left arm around her body. "We'll have to walk quite a bit as the streets near the center don't allow cars."

Another pang went through her. They'd done a lot of walking when they had been together in Atlanta. Only then they'd held hands as they'd strolled, having eyes only for each other. Sometimes those walks had even been cut short by a single look from him that had had them both hurrying back to her apartment.

There would be no holding hands today. Or hurrying home. Elyse gripped her hands together as if her life depended on it.

Maybe it did. Or at the very least her sanity.

She hadn't been able to get that kiss in his office out of her mind. It replayed itself time and time again, ending in that moment when her body had mistaken the signals for something else.

She hadn't explained it to him then, and she wasn't about to attempt an explanation now. Besides, it was better just to let him think that she'd come to her senses. And she had. Just not for the reasons he'd thought.

Despite all of that, it was exhilarating being with him, especially since there'd been a time when she'd thought she'd never lay eyes on him again.

It probably would have been better if she hadn't. His presence threatened to rip apart her defenses, leaving her wondering exactly what lay behind them. She had a feeling she knew. She just didn't want to face it.

She could get through a month, surely.

And meeting his parents? Would she get through that too? What if they tried to send little hints her way that she should marry their son? No. He wouldn't have told them about the proposal, surely.

"You doing okay?" He moved next to her, shoulder brushing over hers as he walked beside her. The brief contact and the concern in his voice left her with a longing that made her ache. He sounded like a concerned husband.

Only he wasn't.

And the sight of him carrying their child?

Oh, God. It looked natural, earthy, his white shirt rolled up over tanned forearms. Italians didn't dress down as much as Americans did, and seeing him in his own environment helped her understand so much about him. Like the fact that he hadn't been trying to impress people with his clothing choices when he'd been in Atlanta. It was just the way he was. His khaki slacks had a fresh-pressed look to them. Probably Emilia's doing, or maybe he took his clothes to a cleaner. But he was lean and devastatingly handsome with his sunglasses pushed on top of his head. Elyse had opted to slide hers down onto her nose, not so much to protect herself from the sun as to provide an additional barrier between them. Or maybe it was to keep him from reading her thoughts.

Evidently, Luca needed no such protection. He was confident and completely unmoved by her. Or was he? There had been moments when she'd been sure that—

"All roads lead to the Duomo."

"Excuse me?"

He grinned at her. "No. I mean literally. All the streets in this area empty out at the cathedral."

"Oh." She hadn't been so much confused by his words as that they'd echoed her thoughts. Because at the time they'd been together all her roads had led to Luca.

And he likely knew it. He had women throwing themselves at him all the time. There were several at the hospital who had given him sideways glances, probably wondering how someone like her had landed someone like Luca.

She couldn't have given them an answer, because she had no idea why he'd chosen her.

And their last act as a couple had been to make Annalisa.

The huge cathedral suddenly loomed in front of them, jerking her thoughts to a standstill.

It was huge. Magnificent.

She touched his arm, wishing she could loop hers through it, just like in days past. "I can't believe I'm standing here looking at something so incredibly gorgeous."

"Neither can I." The low words made her glance over at him. Then she swallowed. And swallowed again, unable to figure out how to keep breathing in and out.

Luca wasn't looking at the church. Or Anna. Or the surrounding area. His gaze was fixed wholly on her.

CHAPTER SEVEN

LUCA'S ARMS CRADLED the baby's body in an effort to keep from reaching out to Elyse. He'd dreamed of bringing her to his home country one day, of showing her the sights, and here they were. But it wasn't quite the way he'd envisioned it. Because in his fantasies they'd had a huge Italian wedding first, with all his family in attendance. And all hers.

Only life and egos and what he'd seen as deception on Elyse's part had changed everything.

But it hadn't been.

She'd said she hadn't been a part of the decision-making process regarding the lay-offs. So this whole time he'd been operating under a faulty assumption. He suddenly looked at her through eyes that weren't quite so cynical—weren't quite so unforgiving.

But did it change anything, really? The

events leading up to the firing hadn't changed. And at the time they hadn't been able to see their way through them.

And now?

"*Scusami. Una foto?*"

He jerked back to reality, realizing someone was trying to take a picture and he and Elyse were in the way. Staring at each other like star-crossed lovers.

"*Mi dispiace.*"

They moved out of the line of fire and headed toward the cathedral itself. He could try to say he'd been looking at something in the distance and not at her, but it would be a lie. And he couldn't bring himself to force out the words. So he just kept walking.

Annalisa chose that moment to wake up, blinking eyes coming up to meet his.

Elyse was there immediately, leaning over to look at her. "I'm here, sweetheart."

His chest contracted. For the last four months, Elyse's face had been the first and last thing his daughter had seen each day. It was as if he hadn't existed.

And whose fault was that? If he hadn't stormed off after they'd had sex that last time—if he'd swallowed his damned Latin pride and come back and demanded she answer his questions about the layoffs and why she was pushing him away—he might have been able to experience his daughter's birth. Her first smile. And she might see him as a parent figure instead of just some random face in the crowd.

Elyse unbuckled their daughter and swung her up into her arms.

She glanced at him, as if realizing something was wrong. "I'm sorry. Why don't you hold her without the sling? She needs to get to know you."

It was as if she'd read his mind. And if the baby started crying?

Well, it was something they would have to work through if he wanted to be a part of her life. And he did. Objectively, it might be easier just to turn away and pretend none of this had ever happened, but he couldn't. Not only because he wanted to do the right thing but also because he already loved her.

In only four days.

It was unreal, but it was true.

He held his arms out and Elyse placed the

baby in them for the umpteenth time. And it was magic. All over again. This was his child. His daughter.

He talked to her in Italian, just muttering things in a long stream of consciousness way that probably wouldn't make any sense to anyone. But he didn't care. There were emotions bottled up inside him that needed an outlet and it was better if Elyse didn't understand the words.

He bounced Anna gently, moving a little distance away. She was listening.

Whether it was five minutes or fifteen, he wasn't sure, but he finally walked back to Elyse, just as Anna started to squirm. "It's okay. Mamma is right here."

"And so is Daddy."

He wished she would stop smiling. Stop seeming soft and approachable again, unlike those last days when her demeanor had been cool and sharp.

There was a part of him that said he wasn't as over her as he'd thought he was. As he'd hoped he was.

He shut those thoughts down as the line started to move, and they had to put Annalisa back in the sling. Then they were finally inside the famed Florence Cathedral.

He wasn't disappointed by her reaction. Elyse gasped when she caught sight of the mosaic floors that were laid out in a grid, each section boasting a new pattern. He tried to see them through her eyes, although it was hard, since patterned streets, sidewalks and the like were such an ordinary part of life in Europe. These were magnificent, however. And they were spotless.

He rocked Annalisa so Elyse could enjoy the sights without interruption. And she did, even as they moved along with the crowds. The tour groups were instructed not to linger so that everyone got a chance to see it. And even though their party was small enough that they weren't required to join one of the groups, he could tell Elyse was trying to be considerate of those behind them. Keeping his voice hushed as was the custom inside, he said, "It's beautiful at night with the lights. Maybe after our meal we can come back and look."

"I'd love that."

"Do you want to climb to the cupola?" She glanced at Annalisa. "I don't think so.

Not with her. I'm just happy to have been able to see the inside. The floors and ceilings are beyond anything I could have imagined."

The wave of tourists washed them back toward the exit, the crowd pinching together as it neared the doorway.

There was a sudden staccato burst of sound up ahead and then a scream of pain. Everyone froze for a second, then someone behind Luca shoved his shoulder and forced his way past. Someone else did the same. The crowd came to life, and what had been a steady procession became a frenzied rush as more and more people struggled to get to the exit.

Luca hadn't thought it sounded like gunfire, although in this day and age he couldn't rule it out.

He grabbed Elyse's hand when it looked like they might be separated, keeping his arm curled around Anna to keep her from being crushed against those in front of him. "Stay close!"

She did, letting go of his hand and wrapping one arm around his waist and gripping his sleeve with the other. They got to the doorway and Luca got a glimpse of something he recognized. A walker. Flattened as if it had been folded and lying on the floor. And next to it...

Oh, hell. He braced himself and stopped, using his body to force those behind him to flow around. Elyse saw it at the same time he did.

Blood. And gray hair.

"God! We have to help her."

"Take Anna and go. I'll see if I can at least keep them off her until help comes. Tell anyone you see who looks official what's happened."

It wasn't easy, but they managed to get the baby out of the sling, and Elyse took her, doing her best to maintain her footing as she was swept through the doors along with the stream of tourists. He didn't dare kneel to check the victim; instead, he turned to face those still coming toward him, making himself as big as possible and shouting at those who would have shoved him aside, first in Italian and then in English. "Go around! There's an injured woman."

It worked. He kept shouting for what seemed like an hour, but was probably five minutes before the crowd thinned, slowed and then dissipated. He saw a set of barricades about twenty yards away, holding the people back.

He swiftly knelt to tend to the woman, a nun, her head covering pulled away. Blood came from a split lip and there was also a large gash on her forehead, the blood from which had formed a small puddle on the mosaic. She'd probably lost her footing and been trampled. A security guard hurried over and with him was Elyse.

"Thank you," he said to her. "Are you and the baby okay?"

"We're fine. They've called for a rescue squad."

She must have found someone who spoke English.

He felt for a pulse. It was strong but quicker than he'd like. "She's breathing, but probably has a concussion at the very least."

"Pupils?"

He smiled up at her. "You read my mind."

He opened the woman's eyes one at a time and checked the pupillary reflexes as Elyse knelt on the mosaic floor next to him, still holding the baby.

"They're both reactive. A very good sign." He then ran his hands over her arms and legs, palpating for breaks.

"There."

"What is it?"

The bone in her left leg was pressed against the skin but hadn't pushed through.

He didn't pull away the clothing, just said, "Her femur is broken. It won't take much to become an open fracture. We can't move her until the squad gets here."

"I agree."

Switching to Italian, he explained the situation to the guard. Not to mention there was no way of knowing if there were spinal or internal injuries.

Two other nuns approached. One of them put a hand over her mouth, turning her face toward the other in shock.

"It's Sister Maria. She fell behind our group. We're visiting from Rome. We had no idea she was hurt."

Elyse stood, putting her hand on the stricken nun's shoulder. "Help is coming."

The guard asked how many were in their party.

The one who'd spoken up answered. "There are two more sisters outside. They're waiting to see if we could find Maria. Will she be all right?"

Maria's eyes flickered and then opened, and she moaned, even as she tried to shift, one hand trying to reach her leg.

Luca pressed gently against her shoulder. "Lie still. You've been hurt. I'm Dr. Venezio and this is Dr. Tenner. We're going to stay with you until help arrives. Does anything hurt besides your leg?"

The woman closed her eyes for a minute, maybe taking stock of the different parts of her body. "My head. The fingers of my hand." She raised it to show digits that were swollen and purple.

He winced. How many shoes had trodden on that frail hand? Thank God Elyse had made it out with the baby. The same thing might have happened to her. Gently taking the nun's hand, he felt it, stopping when she gasped. He reassured her and then turned to Elyse.

"They'll need to get an X-ray to be sure, I can't feel past the edema."

Elyse nodded. "Could be crush injuries.

They'll need to watch for compartment syndrome."

"I agree."

He'd forgotten how well they worked together. Most times, anyway. He glanced at Anna, surprised to see she was silently taking it all in.

A team pushing a stretcher hurried toward them. Luca quickly went through who they were and what they knew about the patient. "Trampling incident. She has a fractured left femur, which needs to be splinted. She'll probably also need her spine stabilized and a neck brace. Vitals are good, but she's complaining of pain in her head and her hand is pretty swollen, there may be a bleeder in there."

One of the techs was trying to get everything down while the other one gathered the necessary equipment from his bag. With Luca guiding the process with some input from Elyse, they soon had Maria loaded while someone went to find the other nuns, who were waiting outside, to let them know what had happened.

And then they were gone, leaving Luca to stand and reach down a hand to help Elyse up, as she was still holding Anna. They went outside before the barricades were taken down and watched to make sure there were no other incidents.

"Well, that wasn't how I expected the tour to end," he said.

"I'm just glad no one else was hurt. Trampling incidents can be horrific. She's lucky she's alive."

"Yes, she is." Something made him drape his arm around her shoulders and give her a quick squeeze. Maybe just thankfulness that it hadn't been her or Anna who'd been injured, even though he was sorry that anyone had been caught in that. All he could assume was that the walker had toppled over, hitting the hard floor a couple of times. The sound of it could have made people jump to the worst possible conclusion and panic, especially when combined with the screaming. As a result, an innocent woman had been badly hurt.

Elyse laid her head on his shoulder, sending warmth washing through his chest. He tightened his grip. Never in his wildest dreams about her had he pictured this scenario.

But he liked it. A little too much.

"You're still wearing Anna's baby sling, you know. I think you got a couple of sideways looks from those guards."

"Let them look. I'm proud to wear it."

"Are you?" She glanced up at him for a moment and there was something in those big eyes of hers that made him wish for impossible things.

He didn't think she'd want to know what he'd really like to do. What being with her right now was making him think. And adding that smile à la Elyse? It was deadlier than any aphrodisiac known to man. No little blue pills needed.

"I am."

Standing outside the cathedral once more, he glanced at his watch. Five thirty. It was still early by Italian standards, but maybe they could get into a restaurant without the normal crush of people. He actually knew of a place closer to the clinic that a lot of the staff went to. It would also give them a chance to swing by the house before they ate and change their clothes. He let go of her and held his arms out for the baby. "Are you hungry? I thought we might go out to eat early."

"That sounds wonderful."

When they got back to the house, Emilia was still there and insisted on staying to watch the baby while they went out and had an uninterrupted meal.

"Do not hurry back. I not hold baby since... my babies... " She held her hands to show how little they'd been, then reached out for Anna.

It was hard to say no when she so obviously enjoyed cuddling Annalisa in her arms. She dropped into one of Luca's recliners, which had a rocking feature.

He pulled Elyse aside. "She'll be fine, I promise. And Emilia will call my cell if there are any problems."

"I trust her. And I need to buy more diapers, since I'm close to running out of the supply I brought with me. Can we stop by a grocery store?"

"Yes. Of course. I should have thought of that."

"Some things don't cross your mind until it becomes a necessity."

He puzzled through the words. Was she only

talking about diapers? Or was there another meaning behind the words.

Regardless, it was true. He'd just instituted a new rule of no touching when it came to Elyse, born out of necessity. Having his arm around her outside the Duomo had made him realize how dangerous it was to touch her, even when it started out innocently enough.

They said goodbye to Emilia and headed out in the car.

"Should we bring something back for her?"

"She'll have already prepared a meal and put it in the fridge. There is usually a lot of leftover food. I normally send some of it home with her, so she knows to eat what she wants."

"Oh, no. I didn't realize she was cooking something for us tonight."

"We'll eat it tomorrow. It's fine."

"If you're sure. How long has she been with you?"

"She is actually one of my parents' house-keepers. She's been with them for more years than I can remember. When I came back to Italy, she volunteered to come and make sure I didn't starve—my mom's words."

"I guarantee you won't. Not with the way

she cooks." She paused, then added, "What happens if you leave again?"

Was she talking about her suggestion that he move back to the States? He loved his work at the clinic—felt like he was doing a lot of good where he was.

But he also loved his daughter. Wouldn't he move heaven and earth for the chance to be with her?

Yes, he would.

"If I left, she would probably opt to go back to my parents." His mother and father were wealthy, his father managing his own shipping company. "She's part of the family. They love her."

She laughed. "Your parents sound like great people. I'm still a little nervous about meeting them, though. Especially under these circumstances."

He could understand that. He was still a little worried about their reaction himself. But probably not for the same reasons she was.

"You'll like them. And they'll love you."

"As much as they love Emilia?" She smiled as she said it.

"More."

She blew out a breath. "Did you tell them after we talked last time?"

He knew she was referring to Anna. "Not yet. I've been thinking through my approach."

"If we just show up with her in tow, that conversation might prove to be a little more difficult."

She was right. He couldn't just spring it on them and pray for the best. Especially not if Elyse was in the room. His parents needed time to digest the information and plan how they were going to approach it before they got there. "I'll do it tonight."

"Good." She looked relieved, getting out of the car and surveying their surroundings. "This is lovely."

"It's close to the clinic and pretty popular."

"I can see why."

They went in and the scents of garlic and mozzarella tickled his nose, making his mouth water. The hum of voices and laughter only added to it. He'd been right to come to Florence. He'd loved the city from the moment he'd set foot into it. There were complaints about the tourists from some quarters, but having lived in another country for over a year he felt a kinship with them that killed a little of the homesickness he'd felt for Atlanta. Even now when he heard a Southern accent from the States, it brought back memories. Good memories of warm food and even warmer people, even if he never had gotten the hang of drinking iced tea.

And if he moved back to the States, he would have to leave his new city behind.

"Luca! *Qui!*" He turned his head and saw Lorenzo motioning them over.

"Dammit." He groaned aloud. "Did I say this was a good idea?"

"Embarrassed to be seen with me?"

There was something in her face that said she really believed he might be.

"What? *Dio*, no. I'd hoped to have a little time alone with you after sharing you with the clinic." He hurried to add, "To discuss our future. With Annalisa." He was making a mess out of this whole thing.

Then again, he'd made a mess out of his relationship with her as well. They might as well join Lorenzo and the other two surgeons at the table. What happened to this being an early time to eat for Italians?

A waitress came up to them, and he mentioned to the trio at the table. "Could we get another chair?"

She brought one and everyone adjusted their places to accommodate them. Even with the moves, Luca found himself squeezed in next to Elyse, knees touching. There was no way to avoid it. When he glanced at Lorenzo, who was on the other side of her, he wondered if her knees were touching his as well. The idea made him subconsciously press a bit closer, an impulse he neither liked nor welcomed.

Giorgino introduced her to the other two doctors, not waiting for Luca to translate. Drs. Fasone and Bergamini each stood to shake her hand.

He told the other two in Italian that Elyse was a surgeon in the US.

Dr. Fasone cocked his head. "What do you specialize in?"

"I'm a neurosurgeon."

Fasone smiled. "Working at a neuro-clinic, you can be fairly sure that many of us are as well."

Coming here had been a huge mistake. The

only married man in the party was Dr. Bergamini.

Why did he even care? He and Elyse were no longer together. It shouldn't matter if she set her sights on someone else.

Well, Lorenzo was a serial dater, out with a new woman almost every week. And Fasone was...well, he was just a nice guy. Someone exactly like Elyse might fall for. He'd certainly be a stable influence on Anna. But that didn't make Luca like it any better.

He was suddenly conscious that his knee was clamped to hers. Unconsciously claiming her for his own?

Dannazione. He needed to get himself together.

He did that by remaining silent while they exchanged stories, with Lorenzo telling the other two doctors about the cavernoma surgery and Elyse's part in it. "It is sometimes good to have an outside perspective, yes?"

Lorenzo smiled at her in a way that made Luca tense.

The server came over and took his and Elyse's orders.

"I'll have whatever you're having," she murmured to Luca. The urge to shoot the other surgeon a look of triumph came and went. He was being childish. She wasn't going to fall for Lorenzo's charm.

He ordered two plates of ravioli with salads on the side, then paused for a second, turning to her. "Salads here come with anchovies. Do you want yours without?"

She blinked. "I've never tried them, but if that's how the salad comes, that's how I'd like mine."

A sliver of pride went through him. Not so much for his homeland but for the fact that Elyse was willing to eat what was common in his culture. "I hope you like it more than I did your sweet tea."

"Didn't I tell you? That's what I'd like to drink with my meal."

This time he laughed. "We have enough tourists that some of the restaurants do serve it. This one, I'm not so sure."

"I was joking. I'm not so sure."

He frowned. "No wine?" In the States she drank wine and Italy was known for its wide array of good ones.

"Not tonight." She gave him a pointed look, and then he realized she couldn't, because of Anna. How stupid could he be? It was too bad. He'd hoped to introduce her to Chianti—produced in the town that bore its name—which was only around fifty miles from here.

"Do they have sparkling water?"

"Yes." He turned to the server. *Acqua frizzante e un chiante.*

Once the server left, he glanced at the men. "You've already ordered?"

"Right before you came in," Lorenzo responded, turning to Elyse once more. "You like the food *dall'Italia?*"

"I love it." This time her knee nudged Luca's twice. She'd sensed the hint of flirtation in Lorenzo's manner and was reassuring him. It was an old game they'd played many times before. If another man so much as looked at her, or if he thought someone was trying to come on to her, she would touch him. Or nudge his knee under the table. Or lay her hand on his thigh to reassure him that she wanted to be there with him. Only him.

That wasn't the case here, but it still helped his muscles release some of their tension. She was telling him she wasn't going to respond to the other man's subtle advances. Luca had never been outwardly jealous, but she'd always been able to sense when he became uneasy.

Drinks were soon poured, and Lorenzo gave a toast in Italian, which Luca translated. "To interesting cases and even more interesting conversation." This time, though, Luca sent the other man a slight frown, which resulted in raised brows on Lorenzo's part. But he helped steer the conversation back to neutral territory, with the other surgeons asking about procedures in the States and comparing them to Italian medicine.

"What was your most disappointing case?" Fasone asked.

This time Luca did tense. He was pretty sure that would be the case that he and Elyse had disagreed on so vehemently and in which they had both been wrong. A simple blood test had ruled it to be something else entirely, but the diagnosis had come too late.

"Well, we had a patient who came in suffering from massive headaches that weren't responding to over-the-counter pain meds. The symptoms led me to suspect a tumor and Luca disagreed, thinking she had a blood clot. An MRI showed we were both wrong. But almost as soon as we wheeled her out of the imaging room, she threw a clot and had a massive stroke. She had polycythemia vera."

Luca added. "Her bone marrow was producing too many blood cells. But they were platelets, not the red blood cells normally found in the condition. It was a rarer form of the disease."

Fasone grimaced. "That's tough. It doesn't sound like you had much hope of saving the patient even if you had diagnosed it from the beginning, though."

"No, she waited too long to come in. She'd been experiencing symptoms for several years and there was already evidence of a couple of previous transient ischemic attacks."

"I'm surprised you two are still talking," Giorgino said with a smile. "Those are the kinds of disagreements that can ruin friendships."

He didn't know the half of it, but Luca forced a shrug. "We were both wrong. So I guess there was no gloating to be done."

Elyse added in a soft voice, "No, there wasn't."

But the disruption of a staff meeting followed by a two-hour argument over whose hypothesis they should follow had damaged their relationship. Not long afterward, the ax had fallen in the form of jobs disappearing.

She'd said she was sorry for that. And he believed her. But did it change anything? In some ways, maybe it did.

Their salads and antipasto came, and the conversation turned to food without him having to force the issue, which he was more than ready to do. If the subject of their breakup was going to be rehashed, he certainly didn't want it to be in front of an audience.

Elyse speared a piece of lettuce and added one of the slivers of anchovies. He waited while she put the bite in her mouth. Her eyes widened.

"Verdict?"

"It's salty. And quite strong. But I like it." She tilted her head and looked at the other surgeons. "So your turn. What were your most disappointing cases?"

They each shared a case that had turned

out badly. One had been human error, but the others had all been just the difficulty of coming up with a speedy diagnosis when things were already heading south. So he and Elyse weren't the only ones who'd lost patients. And the PV case wasn't his only difficult one, but it had been the most dramatic. And the one with the most personal repercussions.

Was there anything he could have done differently?

He wasn't sure. If Elyse hadn't already started to subtly withdraw from him, it might not have become the volcano it had. But she had. In tiny increments he hadn't understood but which had become pronounced after the death of the patient.

Maybe it had been the fact that he and Elyse had worked too closely together. The emotions of their relationship had gotten in the way of how they'd dealt with that patient—he could see that now. It had also got in the way of how they'd responded to each other in the midst of that crisis. Sharp words had cut more deeply. Anger had seemed ten times more significant than it should have.

Her knee had shifted away from his when

talking about the PV patient, but as the others had shared their defeats, she'd relaxed once again.

Her blond hair shimmered in the dimly lit restaurant. And with her expressive face, hands moving as she discussed disease processes, he could see why Lorenzo—or any man, for that matter—would be attracted to her. She had it all. Brains, beauty and an innate kindness that was rare. A man would be a fool not to be drawn to her.

Luca found himself staring at her, loving the way she smiled. And frowned. The sound of her voice. The way she listened intently as she tried to find her way around accents and unfamiliar words.

He pushed his plate away, just as she turned to him. "Do we need to check in with Emilia?"

"Maybe. I'm finished if you are."

"I am."

Luca motioned for the check and paid their bill.

She smiled at the table as they stood. "Thank you for entertaining me. I'm sure there are things you would have preferred to talk about other than medicine."

Bergamini, who'd been the quietest of the bunch, said, "It's always interesting to observe how we deal with difficult diagnoses." He fixed Luca with a stare. "Sometimes we get it right. And sometimes we don't. When that happens, we need to learn from our mistakes. And try not to repeat them."

The man wasn't talking about their cases. No wonder he hadn't said much. He'd been "observing" but it had had nothing to do with medicine and everything to do with relationships. It stood to reason. He'd been married a long time, so he'd obviously figured out how to get it right.

Well, contrary to the man's opinion, Luca *had* learned from his mistakes. He may not have gotten everything right, but he'd come out on the other side with some new ways of dealing with issues.

Mostly that meant not getting involved with the opposite sex. But was that because of the breakup? Or because he was still hung up on the mother of his child?

Soon they were out of the restaurant, the cool air showing the first hints of autumn. By the time Elyse left Italy, temperatures would be dropping at night and staying cooler during the day.

She glanced at him. "Hey. That case we had. It was a hard call. I'm sorry I was so hateful during that."

"You weren't hateful. Just...passionate." He hesitated. "And just so you know, I wasn't aware there was a possibility of a pregnancy that last night or I wouldn't have left, I hope you know that."

He tried to figure out how to express himself. "Our relationship had become like the PV patient: producing an unhealthy amount of tension with no way to drain it off."

Treating polycythemia vera often meant drawing off excess blood in a phlebotomy session. It lowered the red blood cell count, lowering the risk of a heart attack or stroke.

She sighed. "Maybe it's true what they say about business and pleasure. They need to be kept separate."

"With us, there was no way of doing that. We were already involved and both in the same line of work." He smiled. "And that's what drew us together in the first place."

"Really? That's funny, because I was only interested in your…looks."

That made him laugh, since that word had always been her euphemism for something else. "You were, were you?"

She tossed her hair over her shoulder and glanced back at him. "You were always pretty damned good in…the looks department."

The joking faded away, at least on his part. She still thought that? Even after all that had happened? Well, hadn't he just thought about how gorgeous she was a few minutes ago?

The attraction was still there on both sides.

"I was staring at you back in the restaurant, thinking about how heartbreakingly beautiful you are and how I didn't want Lorenzo Giorgino anywhere near you."

She stopped in her tracks and turned to look at him. "Enzo doesn't appeal to me at all. Oh, he's nice enough, and he's certainly good-looking, but I have a feeling he has a serial case of wandering eyes."

Ah, so she had seen through him. "He tends to date a lot of different women. And I don't like it that he has you calling him Enzo."

"You don't?" She smiled. "Well, you don't

have to worry. My sights were always set on a completely different Italian."

Those words hung between them, and Luca moved a few steps closer, stopping right in front of her. "They were?"

"Yes." The whispered word slid through his senses like silk, winding around them and holding them hostage.

He swallowed. "Do I know this Italian?"

"I would hope so." Her palm went to the back of his head, fingers sliding beneath the hair at his nape, sending a shudder through him.

"Because...it's you, Luca."

CHAPTER EIGHT

HIS KISS TOOK her by storm, the awareness that had been bubbling just beneath the surface finally blowing the lid from the pan.

She loved the feel of his mouth on hers.

She always had. She'd ached for him since the day she'd landed in Italy. Long before that, actually.

She wanted him.

Desperately.

She was no longer his boss; there was no need to worry about consequences or what would happen tomorrow. They'd be dealing with each other for the rest of their lives. Wouldn't it be better if they were on good terms?

She shut down the center of her brain that sent out a warning that good terms and sex were not necessarily one and the same.

The kiss deepened, his tongue playing with the seam of her mouth.

God, she wanted to let him in. She pulled back, glancing pointedly at the door to the restaurant. They were still within twenty yards of it. She didn't want Lorenzo or any of the others seeing them. If this was going to happen, she wanted it to be in a place where it was just her...and him. "Let's go somewhere else."

"We can't go home."

Home. Did he even realize he'd said that as if it were her home too? She forced herself not to analyze that too closely. Especially since the word had been said against her lips in a way that pushed her closer to a line she recognized all too well.

"Hotel?"

"They'll be filled with tourists." He stared into her eyes. "How adventurous are you?"

"If you mean sex on a zip line, probably not that adventurous." She smiled. "We could always go back to your office."

"Mmm..." He smiled. "We've done the office bit once before. I was thinking of somewhere a little more intimate. Where we're guaranteed our privacy."

"Sounds promising." She slid her thumb

over his lips. "So where is this mysterious place?"

"My car."

A ripple of excitement went through her. Luca always had brought a hint of danger to his lovemaking, going as far as sliding his hand under her dress once in an empty elevator. He hadn't taken her over the edge but had gotten her so desperate that she'd attacked him as soon as they were back in her apartment.

"And I know the perfect parking place. Are you up for it?"

"Yes." She trusted him not to put her in a position where she would be embarrassed.

He drove a few miles, his hand high on her thigh, reminding her of that encounter in the elevator. But this time he didn't venture any farther. Somehow that heightened her anticipation. Made her want him that much more. Fifteen minutes later, they pulled up in front of a gated house. No lights were on. "Are they home?"

"No, but it doesn't matter. We're not going inside. Reach into the glove box. There's a remote."

She quickly handed it over and watched as

he pushed the button, sending the gates sliding in opposite directions.

"It's a friend's," he said. "I'm watching it for him."

"No cameras?"

"No."

"Ah...so this is what you meant."

"Yes. No one's around." He followed the driveway around to the side, where they were concealed from the nearby houses by a natural screen of vegetation. "The neighbors all know my car, and that I'll be popping in periodically to check on things."

"This probably isn't what your friend had in mind."

He turned off the engine and leaned over to kiss her. "Oh, I plan to check on things."

Lord, those "things" were starting to heat up. The thought of having sex in a car was suddenly the only thing she wanted to do. It was a first. One of many she'd had with this man.

But... She needed to do something before they reached the point of no return. Give him time to back out. Placing her hands on either side of his face, she held him a few inches away from her. "I have to tell you something. The last time we kissed, well… Something happened. Something you need to know about."

He gave her a wolfish grin. "Don't worry. It made some things happen to me as well."

"No, this was…embarrassing. My…um, breasts started tingling. Like when I get ready to nurse Anna."

His eyes widened. "That's why you pulled away?"

She nodded.

"*Dio.* I thought…" He closed his eyes and pressed his forehead to hers. "Never mind. It doesn't matter."

"Are you sure?"

Instead of answering, he leaned over and undid her seat belt, hands going to the bottom of her T-shirt and tugging it over her head. Her bra soon followed. "All I want to think about right now is you. And me. And what we're about to do."

Then he let himself out of the car.

"What are you doing?"

He opened her door and took her hand.

"I thought you said we weren't going inside."

"We're not, but it's a beautiful night. And I want to see you in the moonlight."

She stepped out of the car, trusting him when he closed the door and turned her around. He gathered her hair in his hand and leaned over to kiss her neck. "We're not going any farther than the hood of the car, where we're not cramped, and I can do this." His arms came around her and palmed her breasts, the sweet friction on her nipples making her moan.

"*Dio.* I love the sounds you make. Love what they do to me."

His hands slid over her torso and rounded her hips. Then his fingers walked down the backs of her thighs, the flow of cool air hitting her legs as he scrunched the fabric of her long gauzy skirt in his hands, his teeth still skimming the sides of her neck. It was heady and naughty, and she was frantic with need.

He'd always been good at this.

How she'd missed it. Missed him.

She gasped when he bent her over the hood of the car, which was still warm from the drive over. He braced his hands on either side of her, his hips pressed tight against her bottom.

Giving a shaky laugh, she said, "I don't think the nuns would approve of my attire right now."

"Maybe not, but I approve *con tutto il mio cuore*."

He played with the elastic of her boy-shorts. "I have missed your ridiculous choice of undergarments."

But it was said in a way that was the opposite of ridiculous. Evidently she wasn't the only one who'd missed things. She loved it when he mixed Italian with English. The more caught up he got, the more he reverted to the language of his heart. And it tugged at hers, turning her insides to mush.

Then those shorts were being pushed down. "Step out of them."

Gladly. And when his leg came between hers and urged them apart, she swallowed, spreading for him.

She would be lucky if she lasted until he was inside her. His wallet landed on the car next to her. Just when she was trying to figure out what he was doing, she heard the ripping of foil packaging.

Oh, God, she was so desperate for him, she hadn't even thought of protection—or the fact that she no longer needed it. An arrow ripped through her heart and came out the other side. The pain was short-lived, though, because right now nothing was more important than being with him.

The slow snick of a zipper made her heart pound.

So close.

There was a momentary pause as she imagined him rolling the condom down his length. Then he was back, and one hand slid under her rib cage, finding her nipple without hesitation, pulling hard and strong in rhythmic strokes.

"Ahh..." The sound came out as a long breath of air.

"You make my loins want to explode."

The odd wording would have made her giggle under normal circumstances, but right now she had never felt less like laughing in her life. Her body wound hard and tight with the continued stimulation. She'd never felt anything like this in her life.

She should ask him to slow down, but she didn't want to. Wasn't even sure she was capable of speech right now.

And that spring inside her was slowly twisting, getting closer and closer to the breaking point. She pushed her hips back, finding him briefly only to have him slide back out of reach.

"No!"

"What do you want, *cara*?" he squeezed her nipple and held it tight.

She pressed her lips together to keep from crying out, but the words spilled past the barrier. "I *want* you inside me. Please."

"Yes! *Dio*." His initial thrust was hard and fast, filling her completely.

A second later, she went off, her body contracting crazily around him.

He grabbed her hips and stabbed into her with an intensity that made her breathless and weak.

Then he gave a hoarse shout, before going completely still, straining inside her for several long seconds.

Then he slowly relaxed, curving his body over hers and staying right where he was. He was still for what seemed like an eternity but was probably only minutes.

"Hell, Ellie, that was..."

"I know." His use of that pet name brought tears to her eyes. Ever since she'd arrived, he'd called her Elyse.

Until now.

What had happened to them? How had life become such a damned struggle? But that was then. This was now. So what was holding them back from being together?

He eased out of her and turned her around to face him. He leaned down and gently kissed her, even as he crumpled the empty foil from the condom. That act made the tears that had been teetering on the edge of her lashes overflow their banks.

That. That's what was holding her back. Stopping, he looked at her. "What's wrong?"

She gave him a shaky smile. "Hormones."

It was a lie. But it was all she had.

"You're sure?"

"It's just been a while. I'm good. Just weepy in general." About the fact that they would never again produce a beautiful baby like Anna. That suddenly seemed like the biggest tragedy imaginable.

He nodded as if knowing he needed to give her a little space. Handing her the discarded pieces of clothing, he turned to give her privacy, zipping himself back into his khakis. Hurrying to get dressed, she dried her eyes, grateful to him. And very glad that this had happened here rather than at his place or, worse, at his parents' house. If it had to happen, better for it to be on neutral ground. Ground that she would never see again.

"Thank you," she said.

"For what?"

She wasn't sure. The gift of being with him one more time, maybe? "For not being weirded out by my crazy emotions."

"I have never been, how did you say... 'weirded out' by anything to do with you."

He tipped her chin up. "We are good?"

"Yes. We are." Good, but still not back together. There were no words of undying love. Which she was glad of, right? That would only create complications further down the road that neither of them wanted. His life was here now. And hers was back in the States. Anna was the only thing linking them.

At least for now.

Once their daughter was old enough to travel on her own, they wouldn't need to ever see each other again.

No. She'd already thought this through. There was always Anna's wedding and, later, hopefully grandchildren.

She frowned. Why was she trying to find excuses to see him?

Probably because there was still a part of her that cared about him. That probably always would.

Not a good thing.

Because she was discovering that looking at something through the eyes of passion was a whole lot different than seeing it in the cold light of satiation. And as reality crept up over the horizon and shone down on them, Elyse wondered what this would look like to her tomorrow. The next day. And on the day she actually left Italy—and returned home to Atlanta.

Luca threw a bucket of water over the hood of his car, removing any evidence of what had happened last night. Not that they'd left any marks that he could find. Only the ones burned into his skull.

What the hell had he been thinking?

He didn't know.

They'd wanted each other, there was no doubt about that. But he'd wanted women long before he'd known Elyse and had not acted on that desire. He'd never been one for casual sex that went nowhere. And as it stood right now, his relationship with Elyse would do just that: go nowhere. And tomorrow they were to leave for their trip to Rome.

Elyse had brought Annalisa out for breakfast, but would barely look at him, which was why he'd gone out to wash his vehicle down, thinking maybe the physical act would help him erase the thoughts clogging up his head. He rubbed the hood dry, trying to blot out the heady memories of having her in his arms.

Impossible. They were engraved on his nerve endings and written on his heart. But he was going to have to figure out how to live with those memories or find a way to bury them.

Elyse came into the garage unexpectedly

and glanced at the car before looking back at him. "Could I talk to you for a minute?"

He threw the rag into the bucket and faced her. "Okay."

"I'm not quite sure how to say this."

His sense of foreboding grew. "I find the best way is to just say it."

"About the trip tomorrow…"

"Yes?" Was she going to back out?

"I don't want to share a bedroom with you when we get there."

He sagged against the fender of the car, laughing. "Is that all?"

"I'm not sure why that's funny, but yes."

He glanced up to see a hint of anger in her face.

"No need to worry. My mother wouldn't let us share a room, even if we wanted to. She's *multo* old-school about things. In fact, she attends Mass every Saturday."

Her eyes widened. "Is that what that whole marriage thing was about?"

"Marriage thing?"

"When you asked if it would be easier if we were married?"

This time the anger was on his side. "You

think I'd ask you to marry me as a way to appease Mamma? I would never do such a thing."

"I'm sorry, I just thought——"

"Listen. She would be disappointed if we married for anything other than love. I was wrong to have suggested it."

Her shoulders relaxed. "I'm glad. Because I would be disappointed in myself if I let myself be talked into marriage just to give my child a mother and a father."

He stiffened. "She has a mother and a father. Even without the piece of paper."

And that had not been at all why he'd asked her. Although for the life of him he still wasn't sure what his reasons had been.

"That's not what I meant."

"Then what did you mean?" The words came out sounding stilted and formal, which wasn't how he'd meant them to, but her words stung. She didn't have to convince him that she no longer loved him. It had been obvious that day in the hospital staffroom, when she'd read that list of names and tossed him from her life. And it was obvious now.

"I was talking about sharing the same last name. Anna doesn't care about any of that."

"No. You're probably right." He went on so that she didn't think he was overly bothered by the conversation. "I'm going to be heading to the clinic in about a half hour. Do you want to come with me, or would you rather stay here?"

She didn't answer for a few seconds. Then she said, "Could I come and bring Anna with me? I can put a cot in your office and lay her down for a nap. I really would like to see more of what the clinic does."

He smiled, a few of his muscles uncoiling. At least she hadn't come out here to say that she'd booked a flight out of Italy. He'd call his parents and make his explanations seeing as he'd been too distracted by Elyse to phone them last night. Everything was still on track. At least he hoped it was. Time would tell if it would stay that way.

"How soon do you need me to be ready?"

"I have rounds in around an hour, so...thirty minutes?"

"Sounds good, I'll gather Anna's things."

His gaze skimmed her figure against his

volition. If she noticed she gave no indication of it. "If you just put everything in the living room, I'll load it into the car."

"Thanks. Are you sure you don't mind us coming with you?"

"I'd be disappointed if you didn't."

Keep your enemies close, wasn't that how the saying went?

Only he really hoped Elyse was no longer his enemy. Because by the end of her time here he hoped they could at least be friends.

She was ready in thirty minutes, just as she'd said. But unlike the mountain of things he expected to see on the living-room floor, there was only a collapsible crib and a diaper bag packed with supplies. He glanced at it. "Are you sure you don't want to leave her with Emilia again for a few hours?"

She gave him a sideways glance and said, "No, I think I'd like her with me this time."

Was she afraid he'd try to sweep everything off his desk and take her there like he had on her desk in Atlanta? Or the hood of his car? He'd learned his lesson and wasn't likely to repeat either of those mistakes. Only he wasn't sure the latter *had* been a mistake. There was such a thing as closure. Something he hadn't quite gotten before he'd left Atlanta. Maybe their encounter had been the formal goodbye he'd needed.

He didn't like that idea. At all.

"We can set up the baby cam in my office or use the camera on my laptop to observe her."

"I thought the same thing, so I have the baby monitor in the diaper bag."

"Great. My office door can be locked, but I'd rather be able to check on her from time to time."

"It's just like leaving her to sleep in her room at home. The monitor will alert us to any peeps she might make."

With that settled, he picked up the portable crib and the diaper bag and loaded them into the car while she picked Anna up from the baby blanket she'd spread on the floor.

Emilia came over to kiss the baby on the cheek. "You leave?"

"I'm taking them to the clinic with me. But

don't forget that Elyse and I are going to Rome in the morning," Luca said.

"I no forget. But I miss Annalisa."

He smiled. He was sure his housekeeper would probably miss the baby more than she would him.

"We'll only be there a week."

Elyse shifted and looked away. Maybe "only a week" to her seemed like an eternity. But, for his parents, it would fly by, and he wouldn't be able to tell them when they'd be able to see their granddaughter again.

No, he was sure Elyse would want to work out some kind of schedule. But if he only saw Annalisa once a year, that added up to just eighteen times before she was an adult. The pain that idea caused him was so deep he wasn't sure it would ever go away.

That brought him back to the question he'd asked himself over and over again. If he'd known Elyse was pregnant, would he have still left America?

His response was the same as it had been last time. No. He wouldn't have left.

But she hadn't known at the time, and he

had left, so asking those types of questions caused nothing but torment.

He needed to concentrate on the here and now and figure out a plan for the future. Or he would be left with nothing to look forward to, except recriminations—aimed solely at himself.

CHAPTER NINE

MARY LANDERS HAD had no seizures in the last two days. Elyse gave her hand a quick squeeze. "I'm so glad you're doing well. I hear they're releasing you today."

"Yes, they are. We're going to wait a couple of weeks and then we'll head back to the States. School starts soon, and we don't want our daughter to miss any of it."

Annalisa was sound asleep back in Luca's office. In fact, he'd stayed behind to watch her, not quite comfortable with leaving her alone, despite the baby monitor. She wondered if that was the real explanation or if he simply couldn't get his fill of his daughter.

If so, she knew the feeling.

She couldn't quite get her fill of him. And she was pretty sure she never would. She'd proved that by having sex with him on his car. Her heart had cracked in two over him once before, and the way she was going, it could very well break all over again.

"What grade is your daughter going to be in?"

"Fifth. Bella starts at a new school, so we want to make sure we're back."

The couple only had the one child. Mary had shared that they'd tried to get pregnant again but couldn't. And adoption took so long they'd opted not to go in that route, especially since her husband was in the military, and they might change locations before the process could be completed.

She understood completely. It was something she hadn't told Luca, even after he'd used a condom the other day. In the beginning, she'd kept it to herself because she hadn't thought it was any of his business.

And now?

She wasn't so sure. When she'd gone out to the garage and looked at the car, it had been on the tip of her tongue to tell him. But she'd chickened out.

What would be accomplished by telling him?

"Is she excited?"

"She misses her friends, but since we moved locations and not just schools, it makes it easier. Military kids learn early to cultivate relationships where you find them, because you never know when life will drag you somewhere else entirely."

"I can certainly understand that."

Elyse had a lot in common with those families. Life had changed drastically for her in the space of thirteen months. Her relationship with Luca had ended. Then had come the pregnancy and the resulting hysterectomy. That was about as drastic as it got without someone dying.

On the positive side, she still had her ovaries, so she hadn't been thrown into premature menopause in the midst of everything else.

A hot flash might be a little difficult to explain, and since Luca hadn't taken her skirt off he hadn't even seen her hysterectomy scar, not that he would have surmised that she'd had her uterus removed from that scar alone.

Didn't she owe it to him to tell him? She didn't know. Everything was just a tangle of confusion right now.

"Elyse, could I see you for a moment?"

She whirled around, expecting Luca to be standing in the doorway, leaning sexily against the doorjamb, but no one was there.

"I think it came out of your pocket," Mary said in response to her obvious confusion.

"My...oh, the baby monitor." Luckily it had a two-way speaker feature. She pulled the receiver from her pocket and used it like a walkie-talkie. "What's up, Luca?"

"Anna's hungry. Or something." She suddenly heard the sound of Annalisa crying over the speaker. Luca must have aimed it at the baby, or maybe he was holding her.

"I'll be there in just a minute. Thanks." She dropped the device back in her pocket, a sense of amusement going through her at the tinge of panic that had colored Luca's voice. She remembered feeling that very same fear the first time Anna had cried, when all of the doubts she'd repressed during her pregnancy had come roaring back. What if she wasn't enough for her baby? What if she couldn't get her to stop crying? Or, worse, what if she couldn't tell the difference between something simple and something serious?

So far, she'd dealt with each crying session

as it came and had learned the difference between distress and simple hunger. Despite her difficult pregnancy, Anna had become a relatively healthy baby.

So far, anyway.

She went over and gave Mary's arm a gentle squeeze. "If I'm not here when they release you, take it easy and have a safe flight back."

"Thank you for everything."

She actually hadn't done anything, except to consult with Enzo and give the family some encouragement. But she could imagine how grateful she'd be for a visitor from her homeland if the situation was reversed.

"You and your doctors did all the work. I was only here in case they needed translation work, but Luca could have done that on his own, anyway."

"Luca?"

Ugh, she'd used his first name rather than his title. "Dr. Venezio."

"Oh, yes, of course. He did speak great English. Is Anna your baby?"

"Yes, she is."

"With Dr. Venezio?"

Suddenly she realized that the patient had

added everything up and come to the right conclusion.

Mary was leaving soon, though, so it didn't really matter if she knew.

"Yes, he's her father."

"I thought so. There was something there between you. A couple of looks…"

Her brows went up in surprise. "You were a pretty sick lady when you came in here. I'm surprised you had time to notice anything besides what you were going through."

"I think there was a need to know everything I could about my doctors before I underwent surgery."

"Dr. Giorgino performed your surgery."

"Yes, but Dr. Venezio played a pretty big role in diagnosing it."

"That's true." She paused, then finished the story for her. "Luca and I broke up before I realized I was pregnant."

Mary blinked. "That must be hard, especially working with him." She reached out a hand and Elyse took it. "I hope everything turns out for the best for both of us. This is my husband's last tour of duty and then he plans to use his engineering degree to go into architecture. So let me know if you want a house designed. He's pretty good."

"I will. And thank you." She leaned down and gave the woman a quick hug. "Take care of yourself."

"You too."

And then Elyse left and walked toward the elevators to see what was going on with Luca and her daughter.

When she entered the office, it looked like a tornado had hit. There were three diapers strewn on the floor and Luca was standing in the middle of the room with a big wet mark running down his shirt. "I thought you said she was hungry."

"I thought she was too, but I tried to change her diaper first, like you told me."

"And?"

"We never exactly finished Diapering for Beginners."

Her eyes widened as she realized what the wet spot was. Annalisa had peed on him. She hurried to take the baby. "Oh, Luca, I'm so sorry. I was saying goodbye to Mrs. Landers and lost track of time. I thought the diapers were self-explanatory."

"They are. But trying to hold her and get the diaper situated were harder than I expected."

"It's okay. I remember how hard it was that first time." She dragged the baby blanket over to the discarded diaper, laid her daughter down on top of the barrier and quickly strapped her into it. She glanced around. "Where are her shorts?"

"In the crib. That's where I tried to change her first, then when I couldn't figure it out, I put her on the desk to see if I could get it right."

He hadn't. "At least you tried." She picked up the shorts and stuck one of Annalisa's legs into it and then the other.

The baby stopped crying. Immediately.

Luca dropped into his office chair looking like he'd just been through a particularly difficult surgery. "I'm sorry. I wouldn't have interrupted you if I'd realized."

"It's okay. We were done, anyway." She hesitated, but then decided to come clean just in case Mary let it slip before she left. "Mary guessed that Annalisa was ours."

He frowned. "So?"

"I wasn't sure if you'd want anyone here to know."

"Since Lorenzo was holding her when you two walked into my office, I'm pretty sure someone already does. Besides, I'm not ashamed of her. Or of you. Better to admit everything than to have some twisted version of events travel down the gossip chain."

Admit everything. Something she hadn't exactly done.

Maybe she should take his advice and admit everything.

She touched his hand. "Hey, I think I should—"

There was a knock at the door, and Lorenzo stuck his head in, eyes taking in the scene. "Sorry, am I interrupting something?"

"No." Luca stepped closer to the door. "Did you need something?"

The other man frowned but only hesitated a fraction of a second. "I sent a note asking for a read on a patient this morning, did you get a chance to do it?"

"What time did you send it?"

"Eight this morning."

That would have been around the time she

had gone out to the garage and seen him wiping down his car.

The memory of him bending her over that hood sent heat scorching through her.

Luca glanced at her, head tilting before saying, "I can look now, if you're okay with waiting."

"Yes. I have a consult in about fifteen minutes. The patient is adult. Worsening symptoms since yesterday."

Luca went to his computer, the keys clicking as he looked for whatever it was the surgeon wanted him to see. "Elyse? Care to throw your opinion in as well?"

She went around the desk to find him looking at a series of MRI slides. "Oh, wow."

The images showed a series of lesions in different parts of the brain. "MS?" she asked.

Giorgino nodded. "This is what I thought too."

It looked like a typical case, but there was something…

Luca shook his head. "I don't think so. They're on the basal ganglia. Nothing on the brain stem, like you'd expect with MS." He stared at the images. "Maybe acute disseminated encephalomyelitis?"

"ADEM?" she said. "Yes, it could be."

Similar in many aspects to MS, ADEM often came on after an illness. But it was seen mostly in children, not adults. "How old is she?"

"Fifty-four," said Lorenzo.

"Was she sick recently? Have any type of vaccine?"

The surgeon came around to look at the screen as Luca scrolled back through the medical history. "Nothing."

"Is there someone here with her? A relative, maybe?"

"Suo marito."

Giorgino explained that her very worried husband was down in the waiting area. Calling down to the lobby and asking them to relay the question, they soon had their answer.

"She came down with the shingles virus about a month ago."

Elyse bit her tongue to keep from playing devil's advocate. She hated to be wrong, but in this case she had to admit that Luca probably was correct in his diagnosis. Plus the fact that looking at the scans a little closer, the lesions were more perivenous as opposed to the way multiple sclerosis normally presented. At least this time they hadn't argued about it. Although she might have presented her theory more vehemently if they had been on her home turf, which made her wonder why she hadn't here. Maybe because they weren't as close as they once had been.

Or maybe she'd learned a thing or two since then. If that was the case, something good had come of their last few arguments. Something besides Annalisa.

"Standard treatment, then," she said, "consists of high doses of dexamethasone or methylprednisone to lower inflammation, wouldn't you say?"

Luca and Giorgino suddenly began speaking in rapid Italian that she couldn't keep up with. The surgeon's glance went to her once then back to Luca.

Did they disagree with her treatment plan? Or was the surgeon asking about what she meant to Luca?

No, of course he wasn't. She was being paranoid. They had to be talking about treatment options.

Then Giorgino was gone with a wave and a quick word of thanks.

"Everything okay?"

Luca clicked off the computer screen. "Yes, he went to initiate treatment. He said to tell you thank you."

"That was a pretty long thank you. Besides, you came up with the diagnosis first."

He grinned. "Yes, but I'm not nearly as cute as you are."

"You're a funny guy."

Through it all, Anna had remained quiet as if she knew that they were doing something important. Now that they were done, though, she gurgled, then jammed her hands into her mouth.

"I thought you said she wasn't hungry."

"She shouldn't be. Not yet. And now that the Great Diaper Crisis is over, she should be fine."

"Diaper crisis?"

"Um, you still have a little wet stain on your shirt." A sudden thought made her laugh. "No wonder Enzo looked at us kind of weird. Probably thought something kinky was going on in here."

"Good thing he didn't see us yesterday, then." The sardonic note in his voice stopped her in her tracks.

She guessed what they'd done was a little beyond what they'd experimented with in the past. But it had been incredibly exciting, and she was finding she didn't regret it nearly as much as she should have. "Yes. Good thing."

The moment of telling him she couldn't have kids had come and gone.

"Is the department in Atlanta still downsized?"

The question came out of the blue, taking her by surprise. Was he thinking about her suggestion of moving back to the States? "Yes, unfortunately."

"Why did you stay, then? Afterward?"

"I couldn't leave the patients without anyone there. I know they would have replaced me, but I felt an obligation to them. I still do."

"Even if the hospital works you to death in the process? With those kinds of cutbacks, there's no way you can do justice to the patients that come in."

He was voicing exactly what she'd been thinking. Her voice went very soft. "I know that. But I have to try, while attempting to turn the boat back in the other direction. Sooner or later, they're either going to have to close our trauma center or hire more staff. Because lots of times those trauma cases involve neurological issues."

"Agreed." He touched her hair. "Anna needs you healthy and well. Not a...a wrung-out towel that has nothing left for herself."

"A wrung-out towel?" Is that how he saw her? Not very flattering.

"It doesn't quite come across the same way in English."

"I think I understand what you're trying to say. But since I haven't worked since I had her, I don't know how it's going to be yet. The hospital is using a borrowed surgeon from a sister hospital until I come back online."

"Online. Like a computer program?"

She knew he was trying to help, and she shouldn't be offended, but she didn't like the inference that she would give Annalisa any less than all she had.

And if she really did become a wrung-out towel, like he'd said?

"You have your life together, no bumps in the road, I suppose."

His brows went up. "There have been some very big bumps, especially recently, but as you can see I am making time for both of you."

"As will I when I go back to work."

He nodded. "Very good, then. Let's talk about something else. Like our trip to Rome."

They spent the next twenty minutes discussing their game plan for that first actual meeting. And when they were done, Elyse wasn't sure whether tomorrow was going to be a celebration. Or a wake.

But they would all find out, very soon.

CHAPTER TEN

HIS MOTHER'S GREETING over the phone was filled with warm excitement. "Everything is ready here. I have the ingredients for your favorite meal, ready to prepare. Are you bringing Emilia with you?"

"Not this time, Mamma, but I am bringing someone with me."

"Una fidanzata?"

He cringed at the word fiancée. How exactly did one explain that someone was the mother of your child but not attached to you in any way, shape or form? You didn't.

"Are you sitting down?"

"Don't tell me. You really have chosen someone?"

His mother had been on his case to find a wife for the last several years. Even in medical school she'd asked about girls, despite the fact that the last thing he'd had time for was finding that special someone.

Until he'd met Elyse.

"No. But there was a girl. For a while. In Atlanta. We broke up, but I've since found out that there was…is…a…" He cleared his throat. "A baby involved."

"I don't understand, Lucan. A baby involved in what?"

"She has a child, and that baby is mine."

There was silence over the phone, then he heard her shrieking for his father to come into the room.

Luca held the phone away from his ear to avoid hearing loss.

Dio. He'd known she'd be shocked. Dismayed, maybe. But ultimately he'd thought she'd be happy.

His father must have arrived because he heard rapid-fire voices, but he couldn't make out what they were saying. Then his father came on.

"Luca, what the hell is going on? Mamma says you have a child?"

"Is she okay?"

"She's sobbing."

Damn. She was taking this a lot harder than he'd thought she would. He was glad now that he'd gone into his bedroom to make the call and doubly glad he hadn't waited to tell her upon their arrival in Rome. "I'm sorry, Papà. I only found out myself recently."

"Sorry?" He paused and shouted something to someone, evidently his mother. "I can't hear over her wailing. Why are you sorry?"

"Well... Mamma is crying."

A gust of laughter blew through the line. "She's not crying because she's sad. She's happy. Ecstatic. She was sure this day would never come."

"I'm not married to the baby's mother— and I don't plan on ever getting married to her." That sent a shaft of pain right through his chest. Because at one time he had fantasized about Elyse walking down that aisle. He'd had the ring in a little box in his drawer for a month. He'd held on to it, waiting for the right moment to come. It never had. And now it was stuffed in his sock drawer somewhere, since he'd never had time to return the ring before he'd left for Italy.

"Is she a good girl?"

He blinked at that. "She's a grown woman, Papà, and if you mean is she nice, then, yes, she's very nice. It just didn't work out between us. She flew to Florence to tell me a week ago."

"How old is the baby?"

"Four months, and she's a girl. Annalisa Marie Tenner."

He waited while his dad relayed the information. "Why doesn't she have your last name?"

"Because I wasn't there when she was born. And maybe Elyse wasn't sure what to do about that fact."

He'd assumed she hadn't wanted to give Annalisa his last name because she hadn't been sure how he would react to the news. Or maybe there had been a period of time when she wasn't sure if she would even tell him.

But that was something he could do nothing about at the moment. Maybe later, once they'd come to some sort of understanding and things weren't quite so emotional.

Strike two for having sex with her on the hood of his car. It had muddied the waters and made it hard for him to do anything but think about those last memorable seconds. Because he badly wanted to do it all over again.

And there was no way he could. He needed to keep his head about him, especially now that his parents knew. He didn't want to give them false hope.

Again, his dad stopped to relay the information. "Papà, just put Mamma back on the phone, please."

A minute later, she came on the line, speaking so fast that he could barely understand her. Something about wanting to have a huge party to introduce the baby to the extended family.

Dio! That hadn't been on his radar at all. "Let me talk to Elyse first. She might not want that kind of attention."

"Elyse? This is the mother?"

"Yes. And I'm not sure she's up to one of your parties."

"Of course she is. This is our first grandchild. Everyone must know."

He was pretty sure everyone already did with the way she'd carried on a few moments earlier. "We're only going to be at the house for a week. There won't be time to put anything together."

"Yes, there will. I'll make it work. It can be on your last day at the house." She paused her tirade. "But only a week? How will we get to know either of them in that time?"

He hadn't talked to Elyse about spending more time than that, although she was slated to be in Italy for a month. But he'd been hoping to get to know his daughter a little bit better without his mother hovering over his every move. "She won't be here that long. She's only in Italy for a month and she's been here nearly a week already."

"A month? Spend the rest of the time with us, then."

"No, Mamma, I can't. I have to work. I've already taken a week off as it is."

"We barely see you." The complaint was one his mother always made.

"That's not true. You saw me less than six weeks ago."

"Why don't you come back to Rome and work?"

They'd been over this same argument time and time again. Priscilla believed all her children should be gathered around her. And his sisters were. They had both settled less than ten kilometers from their birthplace. After his breakup, though, Luca hadn't been able to bear the thought of moving back to Rome. His mom was far too intuitive. Between her and his sisters, they would have yanked every last detail from him.

It looked like they might get that chance after all.

"I told you. This clinic specializes in neurology. They're doing great work."

"There are clinics here in Rome as well."

"I'm already here, Mamma. I can't just uproot myself." He paused, not letting his voice run ahead of his mind. He decided to steer her back to one of her original subjects just to save himself. "About the party. Nothing too big. Promise me."

Elyse was going to kill him for throwing her to the sharks, so to speak.

"It will just be family. Maybe fifty people."

"No. That's too big."

"But your aunts, uncles and cousins will be offended if they're not all invited."

"I don't think I even have that many cousins and aunts."

"Oh, at least that many. I can think of a hundred off the top of my head."

Okay, so now fifty was sounding a whole lot better. "Let's not invite all of Rome, Mamma. And I really need to ask Elyse if it's okay. If she says no, we'll have to skip it."

"Ask, then. I'll wait."

"She's probably already asleep. I'll ask her in the morning before we leave and call you then."

He doubted that Elyse was asleep at nine o'clock, but the last thing he wanted to do was knock on her bedroom door and have her answer in pajamas. Or worse.

"Do you promise? Call me early. I have a lot of work to do as far as planning goes."

This time he gave an audible sigh. "Nothing too extravagant. Please, Mamma."

"Of course not. You know me."

Yes, he did, which was why he'd said it. But it really didn't matter. She was going to do whatever she wanted to, and his sisters were probably going to be cheering her on the whole way. Not the way he'd wanted to introduce Elyse to his family. Priscilla had a kind of frenetic energy that others tended to feed off. Either that or they were horrified by it.

She was in her element when planning *festas*. He could remember all the huge Christmas and Easter bashes that she'd hosted. "Just a few family members" quickly became "the" place to be on holidays. Distant relatives finagled invitations just to come and see what his mother had cooked up for that particular celebration. Time to hammer his point home.

"Keep the guest list small. Elyse doesn't speak Italian, so she's going to feel totally out of place as it is."

"I will enlist your father's help. I will tell him to rein me in if I'm getting too...what was the word? *Stravagante.*"

She said it with such a flourish he had to laugh. "You're impossible, but *ti amo*, Mamma. Don't do anything until I call you in the morning."

"I won't, I promise. I love you too, *mio figlio.*"

He hung up the phone and sat on his bed for a minute. Should he ask Elyse tonight?

No, because, again, that would entail him knocking on her bedroom door. Which was probably why his subconscious was pushing for him to do just that.

Well, it could keep pushing all it wanted. This time he wasn't listening.

"She wants to do what?"

Elyse was horrified. Luca's mother wanted to throw a party—for Annalisa—and she knew nobody. Suddenly she wondered if coming to Italy had been a mistake, if everything she was doing here was just going to make things worse. She glanced in the back seat, where Annalisa was sleeping, hoping beyond hope she was doing the right thing.

"It will keep her busy and stop her from asking too many personal questions."

She could just imagine what some of those questions might be. A party didn't sound too bad when you looked at the other possibility. She relaxed in her seat. "I don't even speak Italian."

"I'll translate for you. It's only for relatives, and she's excited about meeting Annalisa. That's what you were worried about, right?"

True. Luca had said his mother was old-fashioned. It would have been worse if she'd wanted to hide Annalisa away and never speak of her to anyone outside Luca's immediate family. But the last time he'd translated for her, she'd been a royal wreck. She'd have to be careful about letting that happen again.

"Yes. Tell her okay. I just don't want to embarrass anyone."

"Elyse, you could never embarrass a soul." She shivered the way she always did when he said her name. His accent combined with that low graveled voice gave the word an exotic sound that got to her. Every single time.

"Oh, believe me, I could. I embarrass myself all the time. In lots of different ways."

He took his hand off the stick shift and touched her knee. "You're an excellent surgeon. And caring and compassionate with your patients."

A smile came up from deep inside her. "Right back at you."

He tilted his head, and she realized he wasn't sure what she meant. His English vocabulary was so extensive that she sometimes forgot there were still things that confused him. "It means that I think you're also an excellent doctor and caring and compassionate with your patients."

He grinned. "In that case, I thank you."

"Your mom knows we're not together?"

His hand went back to the gear stick and she immediately regretted voicing the words. He'd already said he would let his mom know that they had broken up. "Yes, she does."

"Sorry. I just wanted to make sure I wasn't supposed to play your doting wife."

He laughed. "Would you? Play a doting wife, if I asked you to?"

He's joking, Elyse. He doesn't mean anything by it.

"Of course I would." She batted her eyelashes at him in a theatrical sort of way. "Think your mother would believe us?"

"Probably not." He took a turn that put them on the ramp to a highway. "She always knew when I was lying before I even opened my mouth."

"Well, I guess we shouldn't lie about our relationship then, should we?" Which made Elyse a little nervous, since she was no longer certain what was truth and what wasn't. She'd told herself she was over him for so long that she'd come to believe it. But was it the truth? There were moments when the past came blazing through in all its glory and she was sure she'd been wrong about everything. Like after they made love the other day. It had taken everything she had to reason herself out of it.

If Luca asked her today to stay in Italy, stay with him, would she?

He didn't love her.

But what if he did? something inside her whispered.

What if he did?

"So no lies, right?"

The words made her jerk around to look at him. "What?"

"Where were you?"

"Oh, sorry, I was thinking about what to wear to the party."

One of his brows went up and stayed up, but he didn't challenge her words.

No lies? Ha! She was starting out on the right foot with that one.

If his mom was as intuitive as Luca said she was, she was going to have to watch her step before the woman decided she and her son were actually meant for each other. "Go ahead and call her."

"Thank you. She promised it would be a small affair." He pushed a button on his dashboard and she heard a woman's voice answer in Italian. Luca answered in kind and a rapid-fire conversation took place, none of which Elyse understood. But she heard Luca placing emphasis on certain words and his mother answering.

Priscilla—wasn't that her name?—had a melodic voice that Elyse instinctively liked. There was a strength to it, but not the kind that forced its will on anyone.

Within five minutes it was over, and Luca pushed another button. "She said to say thank you and tell you that she loves you already."

Her heart clenched.

"She sounded sweet on the phone, even if I couldn't understand her."

"My sisters are a lot like her."

"Tell me about them." That seemed like a safe enough topic.

"Well, Isabella is a lawyer. She's very smart and intuitive about people."

Another person who would be able to see

right through her. She was starting to get this horrible sense of foreboding about this whole visit. "And the other one?"

"Sarita is the baby. She is studying to be a psychologist. She's in her final year of studies."

A lawyer and a psychologist walk into a bar…and try to figure out the biggest lie of them all: that she no longer loved their brother.

Because she suddenly realized she did. She still loved him, after all this time.

God. How had this happened?

So much for thinking her feelings for him were dead. Obviously that wasn't the case.

Fake it. Fake it good, Elyse.

"So do Sarita and Isabella live in Rome?" Maybe they would only arrive for the party and then head right back out.

"They both do, so you'll get to spend some time with them."

Well, at least he'd mistaken the reason she'd asked. "That will be great. Do they speak English?" Maybe if they couldn't understand her, they wouldn't read between the lines.

"Yes, they both are pretty fluent, unlike my parents, so they can help translate as well."

That was the last thing she wanted. Would her body language immediately give her away? "Great." Time to switch her thoughts to the road in front of them to keep herself from keeling over in shock. Or start to worry that every little thing she said would make him guess the truth. She swallowed, trying to shake the fear away.

"The signs on the highway look so bizarre to me. Did the ones in the States seem strange to you when you were there?" Thank heavens her voice didn't come out as shaky as she felt inside.

"What?"

"Everything being in another language."

He glanced at her. "A little. The worst was getting used to miles instead of kilometers and Fahrenheit instead of Celsius."

"I can see how that would be strange." She licked her lips and reached for another neutral topic. "Italy is gorgeous. I love everything about it."

There was a pause. "Everything?" Had he seen through her already? If she kept on like this, she was doomed. She tried to deflect one question with another. "Did you love everything about At-lanta?"

"Pretty much. Maybe not the traffic, even though we have that here as well."

She ran out of questions, so she sat there and leaned her head against the headrest. Anna was sound asleep in the back, so she focused on the sound of the tires against the roadway, instead of the realization that had shaken her to the core.

Random bits of thought swirled around like the leaves caught in a stiff breeze. She might be able to reach out and catch one of them, but she was too afraid of what she might find written on it. So she let them go on their way, closing her eyes and blocking out everything except for that constant background hum, her limbs slowly relaxing. Gradually getting heavier and heavier.

The swirling stopped, and one leaf drifted downward, settling in the corner of her mind. And on it was a single terrifying word.

Love.

Elyse had seemed distracted ever since they'd arrived at his parents' house. It was understandable, but he was sure there was something else underneath it. That feeling that she'd kept something hidden from him ever since her arrival in Italy.

Well, he hadn't spilled his every thought to her either.

He'd translated the introductions, and she'd responded politely when they made small talk, but he couldn't shake the feeling that something was wrong.

So far the only genuine smile he'd seen on her face had happened when his mother had lifted Anna into her arms and squeezed the baby to her chest, eyes closed, tears pouring down her cheeks. At that moment Elyse had glanced his way and smiled, putting her hand over her trembling lips.

That had been genuine. But it had also been short-lived.

Priscilla, who'd installed herself in an ornate rocking chair, looked up. "Would you show Elyse to her room and carry her bags up? I'll hold the baby."

She wasn't likely to let go of Anna anytime soon. And that was fine with him. It was better than the alternative, which was for her to have given Elyse a much cooler reception.

But she had been warm…effusively warm. His dad had beamed as well. He hadn't had a chance to hold Annalisa yet, but he'd only left his wife's side long enough to bring a pitcher of water and some fruit juice, setting the offerings on a sideboard with some glasses. He wasn't as openly emotional as his wife, but he too was deeply moved by seeing his grandchild for the first time.

He glanced at Elyse. "Are you okay with that?" He wasn't going to assume anything. Not anymore. Especially with the mood she was in.

"I am. But I can get my bags."

He picked them up before she could make a move. "I've got them. Care to follow me?"

Leading the way up the stairwell, he glanced back and saw her hand reach for the banister and grip it tight.

Hell, she was shaking.

"They love her." If that's what she was worried about, he wanted to set her mind at ease. "I told you they would. She's their granddaughter. Even if she wasn't, they would still love her."

"She's yours. I swear."

He reached the landing and turned around quickly, which made her pause a couple of steps from the top. "Have I ever implied that I thought she wasn't mine?"

"No, but I could understand how——"

"I know she's mine. I don't need a test to tell me that. I never did. I *know* you. Know I was the only one you were involved with, even if we weren't always getting along very well." He set the bags down and went to her, cupping her elbows. "She has your eyes, but I definitely see a melding of the two of us when I look at her."

"So do I." She wrapped her arms around his midsection and laid her head on his chest. The move left him glued in his spot.

"I wish…" She sighed. "I guess it doesn't matter what I wish. It is what it is, and we just have to do the best we can."

He rested his chin on her hair, closing his eyes. He'd missed these moments. Suddenly her arms dropped back to her sides and he felt that slow withdrawal that had happened so many times toward the end of their relationship, when he'd been left wondering what had gone wrong.

Dammit. Turning, he started back up the stairs.

They stopped at the end of a long hall of closed doors. This door in front of them was also shut tight. "This is yours. Mine is right across the hallway."

She gave a quick laugh. "I would have thought they'd have put us as far apart as possible. Maybe even on different floors."

"No, it would have been you who did that."

He couldn't resist throwing out a reference to a distance that was so much more than physical.

"What do you mean?"

He wasn't touching that question, because he might say something he regretted. "You're the one who insisted on separate bedrooms."

"I know." She muttered something under her breath before pushing open the door. Her breath came out in a whoosh of sound. "Luca, it's beautiful."

The room was big, as were all the bedrooms.

And directly across from them was a huge four-poster bed carved from mahogany.

"I'm glad you like it."

He set her bags on the floor just inside the door. He nodded over at a matching tall dresser. "The drawers will be empty. Feel free to unpack."

"Will your mom be okay with Annalisa for a while?"

"Of course. I'm sure she's hoping we'll be a while."

He realized how that sounded when something flashed in her eyes, and she was suddenly back from wherever she'd gone, wholly present, wholly accessible.

Unsure how long this reprieve was going to last, his gaze trailed over her features before settling on her lips.

She'd fallen for him at one time.

And what about now?

If he kissed her, would she kiss him back?

Would they slam the door and fall onto that tall bed and make love?

If he stood here much longer, he was going to do exactly that. So it was time to leave.

And fast.

Before he put his thoughts to the test and gave his mother a false sense of hope. Because even if he would have liked another chance to work things out, it was doubtful that Elyse would. Despite that one episode on the hood of his car.

"Do you want anything before I go?" His lips tightened when those words were as blundered as the last ones.

"No. Nothing, thanks. I'll be down in a few minutes."

He took that as a dismissal and was through the door in an instant, closing it behind him before he said something he'd regret. Something that could never be erased.

Heading back the way he had come, he threw one last glance at the dark wooden surface of the door and wondered if she knew.

Wondered if she realized that as he'd stood there wishing he could kiss her, he'd almost muttered the phrase he'd held back that night in Atlanta.

He loved her. Had never stopped loving her. And, hell, if it wasn't going to be his undoing.

Because there was nothing he could do—no deity he could implore—that could erase what was now burned onto his very soul.

CHAPTER ELEVEN

THE PARTY HAD been organized for tonight, the penultimate night of their stay, which was both good and bad. It was good in that she'd barely seen Luca the evening before except for dinner. Elyse wondered if he was making himself scarce on purpose, which would be good for her. Except she didn't seem to feel that way.

This morning, though, he'd met her for breakfast and said he'd show her around the grounds. "If you need some privacy, there's a small *terrazza* a little way from the house, which is where I used to go as a kid. I built a fort there for just that reason, in fact."

"Wow, is it still there?" Somehow she couldn't imagine Luca needing to get away from anyone. He was self-assured and confident. She was pretty sure he hadn't suddenly gained those characteristics the second he'd become an adult.

"The *terrazza*. Yes, it's still there. The fort? No, it's long gone. It was made out of a collection of cardboard boxes. It even had different rooms."

"I somehow can't imagine you making a play fort."

He tilted his head. "Why not? Don't most kids?"

"Yes, I made my share in the house. Blankets over the dining-room table. I didn't quite get as ambitious as you did. I just wanted to have a secret place to read."

"So did I."

That was another thing that surprised her. She'd pictured him playing soccer and doing sports, not being a kid with his nose stuck in a book. "You liked to read?"

"Loved it. Especially adventure stories. I loved danger."

Now, *that* she could see. Maybe the danger in those books had infused itself into his being, because she couldn't imagine a man more dangerous to her senses than Luca was.

Before she could think of an answer that was as far from that thought as she could get, Priscilla swept into the room and said something, which Luca translated as a greeting. Then she and her son had a quick argument, and his mom gave him a frown and looked at Elyse and said something in Italian. When Luca didn't explain, she said in broken English. "Please say her."

Luca sighed. "She wants to know if she can take Annalisa into town and get her a new dress. I told her she has all the clothes she can possibly use, but Mamma wants her to have something that's from her. For the party." He looked in her eyes. "If you don't want her to, I'll explain that."

"Heavens. Of course she wants Annalisa to have something new for the party. It's fine. I have a bottle ready in the fridge for her."

When he relayed that back to Priscilla, she smiled, setting off a dizzying array of crinkles beside her eyes that really brought out the beauty in her face. Luca looked like her. So did Annalisa, if she was honest.

An hour later the two were out the door, leaving Elyse almost alone in the house with Luca, since his father had gone to work for the day.

The housekeeper was there, but she was busy with the caterers and other professionals who were getting things ready for the party that night. Luca had promised her it would be a small affair but, seeing the crew in action, somehow she didn't believe him. Who hired caterers for dinner with the family? And something about the way Luca had said "party" when he'd first talked to her about it made her think it wasn't going to be as simple as he made it out to be. All she could do was smile and hope for the best.

"Do you want to go for a walk? I can show you the actual garden where treasures were smuggled and dragons were slain."

That made her laugh. "Well, when you put it that way, how could I refuse?"

He led her down a mown path, the splash of flowers on either side of them looking wild and free. The funny thing was, those flowers had probably been carefully tended to do exactly what the gardener wanted.

"So where was this magnificent fort?"

"Right here."

The flowers had given way to an open cobblestoned area that had a couple of benches. Off to the side was a crystal clear pond that bubbled with fish and water plants. "Your parents let you have a cardboard village in the middle of all of this beauty? How long was it here?"

"A couple of years on and off. My sisters tended to tear it down almost as fast as I could build it. This is where they brought their friends, and they certainly didn't want their brother messing things up for them."

She could picture that scene happening. Since she was an only child, she hadn't had any of the competition that faced siblings.

"They probably brought their boyfriends here later. It's the perfect place."

"Yes. It is. And they did."

She didn't want to ask, but she couldn't help it. "And you. Did you bring your girlfriends here?"

"Hmm… I can remember a time or two."

"A time or two? I bet you had them swarming over you."

He motioned her to a bench and then sat next to her. "No. No swarming. I've never been one to play around."

"No. You never were." Memories of them colored so many parts of her brain that she was pretty sure he'd traveled along most of her synapses.

He turned toward her. "Thank you."

"For what?"

"I don't know, exactly. Annalisa. The crazy times we had. Something beautiful came from what I'd always seen as scorched earth."

"Oh, Luca. I feel the same way. If we'd never gotten together...never had that fight in my office...she wouldn't be here."

His fingers touched her face. "We built our own fort and hid away in it for a while, didn't we?"

"Yes, we did."

Dark eyes stared into hers. "Is it completely gone?"

She could lie. Or she could tell the truth. Hadn't they agreed not to lie to each other?

"No," she whispered. "It's not."

He exhaled heavily. "I so needed to hear that." His palms skimmed her jawline. "Because I don't think it is either."

Then his mouth was on hers in a kiss that tested the whole scorched-earth theory, because it was still as beautiful and wild as those flowers they'd passed on their way here.

He stood and held his hand out to her, and there was no hesitation when she answered his invitation. Two minutes later they were in her room in that big bed, where he undressed her. Slowly. Carefully.

So different from the car experience, where things had been removed in frantic haste, but this was no less fulfilling. They explored each other, relearning curves and planes, seeking out subtle changes that had taken place over those lost months. He found her scar, but even as she stiffened, he shushed her.

"It's beautiful. This is where my Anna came into the world."

He made her feel cherished and cared about.

And maybe even...loved?

Did he love her?

She swallowed. *Did he?*

Ask. Do it.

She couldn't make the words form on her lips, so she decided to show him instead, in the hope that he would whisper the words she longed to hear.

Instead, he climbed off the bed and pulled his wallet from his trousers and laid it on the bed. She closed her eyes, knowing exactly what that represented.

It didn't matter. She could tell him later. Once she knew for sure how he felt. Maybe he wouldn't need more kids. Maybe he'd be okay with just one. Just their Anna.

He went into the attached bathroom and when he returned he didn't have a stitch of clothes on. But he did have a small towel.

The question was almost lost when he climbed on the bed and straddled her. Then she found it. "What is the towel for?"

"I'm glad you asked." His smile was wicked. "Because I'm about to show you."

He draped the towel over her chest, covering both breasts. At first she thought he was worried about her modesty, until he gripped either end of the towel and slowly drew it back and forth over her. The thick terry teased the nipples underneath, creating a kaleidoscope of sensation that soon had her writhing on the bed.

"Ah… Luca, I'm not sure…" The words ended on a moan when he increased the downward pressure as he continued to seesaw the towel, over her, driving her wild.

Her hips bucked under him, but his weight on her upper thighs kept her from getting any kind of satisfaction. He leaned down next to her ear. *"Ti voglio così tanto bene."*

Was he saying he loved her?

Didn't know. Didn't care.

The towel stopped, making her eyes open. "Don't worry, Ellie. I'm not done yet. Not by a long shot."

Picking up his wallet, he opened it, started to draw out a condom.

She stopped him with a hand on his. "We don't need one."

That was as close as she could get to the truth. She could explain it all later, but right now she just wanted to feel him. All of him.

"Dio. Cara. Yes. I want that too. You don't know how much." He leaned down and took her mouth in a kiss that sent pretty little lights spinning behind her eyes.

Then the weight came off her thighs, freeing her for a second or two, before he gripped her hips and turned them so that she was where he had been. On top. Positioned in the perfect spot.

She went still for several seconds, poised on the very edge of heaven and not quite sure how she'd gotten there, or what she'd done to deserve it.

"Do it." His hands tightened on her hips, but he didn't try to yank her down. "Please."

Instead of taking him in a hurry, she eased down, feeling each silky inch of him as she took him in.

He muttered those words that meant nothing and yet told her everything she wanted to hear as she rocked her hips, retracing her path up and then sliding back to the bottom.

There was something unhurried and yet desperately rushed in her movements, and she couldn't quite choose one or the other. Until one hand covered her breast and the other tangled in her hair, pulling her toward his mouth. The combination of the friction of his palm and his tongue over hers made the decision for her. Her movements quickened, and she suddenly didn't care about anything other than how he was making her feel.

Up and down. Empty and full. She couldn't get enough. And when his fingers slid out of her hair and worked their magic elsewhere, she lost it, pushing down hard and then pumping to an internal rhythm. She climaxed, crying out against his mouth, even as he flipped her onto her back and drove into her again and again until he lost himself inside her.

There were several moments when she felt suspended in space. Untethered. Floating free.

Loved.

He hadn't questioned her decision about the condom. Had seemed to embrace it.

That had to mean something. Didn't it?

A single worry reappeared, joined by a second. Then a third.

She opened her eyes to find him watching her. She searched for something to say. "How long before your mom gets back?"

Groaning, he kissed her cheek. "I have no idea, but…"

She laughed. "You don't want to be caught necking in the back seat?"

"But we're not in a back seat. We're in bed."

God, she loved him. Loved these little differences that gave their world color and dimension. "It means we don't want to be caught together. In bed."

His nose nuzzled her ear. "I don't want to go."

"I don't want you to go either. But eventually someone is going to come looking for us. And when they do, I'd rather be fully clothed. And in our separate rooms."

He rolled off her, drawing her into his arms. "Okay. I'll go. But only because I don't want Mamma's party guests to go home with any salacious tales."

"Salacious?" That was suddenly her new favorite word.

"Yes. Of what we were making in this room." He got out of bed and leaned over her. "And just so you know, I do want more."

And then he was gone, leaving her with a tingle in her belly that wouldn't quit.

He wanted more.

Just the thought made her want to go find him and snatch him back to the room or to their fort or whatever they wanted to call it. As long as they were together.

With a joy she hadn't felt in a long time—one that was different from the day-to-day happiness that Anna gave her—she got up to shower and dress for the party.

CHAPTER TWELVE

HE HELD HER hand for most of the evening, trying to give her a boost of confidence while people spoke Italian all around them. Although he wasn't sure if the hand holding was for her…or for him. Those moments in the bedroom had been beyond anything he could have imagined, and they hadn't had a chance to talk about it.

She hadn't wanted to use a condom. Surely that meant she wanted a fresh start together? And more children. He'd made sure she knew he was in favor of that by whispering that he too wanted more.

She loved him, he was sure of it. Even if she hadn't said the words.

Then again, neither had he. But he would. Very soon.

He expected his mother to say something about all of this hand-holding, but she seemed oblivious. Everyone's attention was riveted on Annalisa, who was taking everything in her stride much better than she should have as she was passed from person to person.

"Are you okay?" Hell, he hoped he wasn't just imagining things.

She turned to him with a smile. "I am. For the first time in over a year." She nodded toward Anna. "She looks adorable in that dress your mom found."

"She has a knack for finding the perfect gift."

Anna was wearing a mint-green dress, complete with tulle around the full skirt and a satin bodice. She looked like a princess from a movie. She even had a tiny glittering tiara perched on her head. Luca had no idea how they'd kept her from knocking it off. But she hadn't. She was smiling and cooing and generally being the most beautiful thing he could imagine.

Other than Elyse.

While she wasn't wearing mint green to match her daughter, she did have on a black dress that ended just above the knee, her shoulders bare and tempting, her hair swept up into some kind of fancy knot with strands that wound their way down the sides of her face and tickled her nape. And she had on these high heels that made him think of things that were better off left unthought.

"Oh, I almost forgot! I brought that wine for your mom. We were going to get the flowers here, remember?"

"We can do that first thing tomorrow morning."

She licked her lips. "So your mom would definitely be scandalized if we shared a room?"

Two days ago he wouldn't have been able to envision a scenario where that kind of a question would come up. Or even thought. But he liked it...wanted things to keep moving in this direction.

"Ellie, I'm surprised at you." He gave her a grin. "In the best possible way. But yes. She probably would, although if I happen to have a nightmare involving the two of us kissing, and sneak into your room for comfort..."

She giggled. "A nightmare? Really? Should I be insulted?"

"Perhaps nightmare was a poor choice of word."

"I should think so." But she said it with a smile. And Elyse seemed...happy. He couldn't remember seeing her this way since...well, when there had still been some good in their relationship.

Her eyes trailed their daughter as she was handed over to yet another family member.

"Do you want me to bring her to you?"

"No, she looks happy."

"And how about you?"

Her brows went up and she leaned her head on his shoulder for a second. "What do you think?"

He noticed his mother was finally staring at them, and he had a fleeting thought that maybe they shouldn't be putting on a display of affection in front of everyone until they worked out the rest of their differences, but he wasn't about to push her away.

It was okay. Elyse was relaxed, and if she didn't care about his mother mentally putting rings on their fingers, then he shouldn't worry about it either. But he did have second thoughts about sneaking to her room tonight.

If he was serious about doing this thing, then he wanted to do it right, not rush her into anything. His own prideful determination had messed up their relationship once before. He wasn't about to let that happen again.

Hopefully, if things went well, there would be many, many more moments like these. Slow, easy moments that led to something strong and lasting. And if it meant him moving back to America to get there, then so be it.

Elyse's arm flapped around on the bed beside her for a minute. Empty. A flicker of disappointment was quickly extinguished.

So what if he hadn't come to her room as he'd suggested he might? It had been a long evening. He had probably been exhausted. Just as she had been.

Cracking open her eyes and stretching, she couldn't stop a smile from forming. She'd been hoping to talk to him about the reality of her situation and why they hadn't needed to use that condom, something she hadn't been able to say when they had been making love. He cared about her. She'd felt it brewing under the surface yesterday. His words had seemed to confirm that fact, but she wanted him to go into this relationship—if he even wanted one—with his eyes wide open. This time there would be no holding back or letting things fester and foment.

He'd held her hand last night. In front of his mom, his relatives and everyone. That meant something.

She glanced at her watch. It was barely seven o'clock and it was their last full day here. Climbing out of bed, she jumped in the shower, lathering up in record time. Maybe she could still catch him and have that talk before breakfast, if he hadn't already gone downstairs. Or maybe when they went to buy those flowers he'd talked about as a thank-you present for his mom for hosting her. There was still time. She was sure of it.

With her hair damp, and her face washed clean, she found the bottle of Chianti and dropped it into the red silk wine bag they'd bought to go with the flowers and put it on the mahogany dresser. She ran her fingers over the ornate lines that looked so at home in this room. Her glance snagged on the crib, where Annalisa was still fast asleep. Last night had worn her out. Her daughter didn't normally stay awake that late, but it had been a special night, and she'd fallen asleep in her grandmother's arms, bringing a lump to Elyse's throat and an ache to her heart. Suddenly a week with them seemed like no time at all.

You need to find Luca. Maybe you can work something out.

She went across the hall and softly tapped on his door, hoping that if the rest of the household was still asleep she wouldn't wake them. When there was no answer, she knocked a little louder. "Luca?"

Still no answer. She pursed her lips to the side. He could be in the shower. Or he could already be downstairs. She went back over and peeked in her room. Anna was still out. She'd nursed right before going to bed last night, so she could zip downstairs, find Luca and ask him if they could talk.

Tiptoeing down the treads, she stopped when she heard voices coming from the kitchen. One of them was Luca's. He was talking to a woman and sounded...concerned. Or something. Since he was speaking in rapid Italian she wasn't sure if she was reading him right. She started to turn and go back up the stairs but then the housekeeper appeared in the doorway and smiled at her, motioning her forward.

Ugh. But she was going to have to face him sometime. Except all the hopeful thoughts she'd had moments earlier were now faltering. Who was he talking to?

She forced herself to breeze through the door with a smile, hoping it didn't look like she'd been skulking in the doorway. Luca and his mother saw her at the same time, and the conversation immediately went silent.

They'd been talking about her. She swallowed. Maybe his mother had seen them last night and decided she didn't want her son taking up with someone from a different culture.

No. Things like that didn't happen anymore, did they?

She forced herself to speak, even though her throat felt packed with sawdust. "Good morning. How is everyone?"

Luca came over to her with a smile, throwing another glance toward his mom. He gave a quick shake of his head.

He didn't want her telling Elyse what they'd been discussing.

The sawdust turned to glass. Was it about Annalisa? Were they plotting how they were going to get her to spend more time in Italy? *You're being ridiculous. And paranoid.*

His mom came over and took her hands, holding them up and kissing one. She winked at her son then turned her attention back to Elyse.

"Mamma..." Luca's voice was full of warning.

"Pssht."

Her response made Elyse's eyebrows go up. When they came back down they were contracted into a frown. "What's going on?"

Priscilla gave her hands a gentle squeeze. "You give Luca more babies?"

Babies?

The pain that stabbed her insides was sudden and intense, like the scars from her surgery when they had been new and raw. "Wh-what?"

Suddenly Luca's words from last night took on a whole new meaning.

Just so you know, I do want more.

Was that what he'd meant? He hadn't just been talking about making love?

God. Hadn't he mentioned changing his mind about having children? She could have sworn the word "maybe" had been in there, though.

Had he talked to his mother about it before discussing it properly with her?

Luca came over and touched his mom's arm, saying something that made her let go of Elyse's hands and turn toward him. "She love..." the woman tilted her head as if trying to find the right words. "She love you."

His mom's gaze swung back to her.

She expected Elyse to respond? What could she say, when this went to the very heart of her fears?

Of course Luca would want more children. And she'd fostered that expectation by saying they didn't need to use a condom. No wonder he'd seemed so happy about it. He'd thought they were on the same page.

Oh, how wrong he was.

He and his mom had been talking about children and families. And they had left her completely out of the conversation.

What would happen if he knew she couldn't have any more?

That wasn't something she was going to discuss in front of anyone else. And suddenly she didn't want to discuss it with Luca either. Not now. Maybe not ever.

Hurt and regret streamed through her system. If he hadn't left and had been beside her during her pregnancy, he would have known exactly what she'd gone through. The heartbreak of finding out she could never have another child.

But he knew none of it. And she hadn't told him when she'd had the chance, allowing things to become twisted beyond repair. Just like they had in Atlanta.

"Ellie, are you okay?"

The room was blinking in and out of focus, and she realized tears were very near. She could answer his mom's questions truthfully, if she chose to: Yes, she loved her son. And, no, she wouldn't be having any more of his babies.

"I'm fine." She forced a smile, desperately needing to escape. "We'll have to sit down and talk about that. But I think Annalisa is about ready to get up."

"I'll come up with you," Luca said.

"No." She snatched a quick breath. "I'll bring her down in a few minutes, once I've fed her."

His mom came over, her smile gone. "You cross…" she pointed at herself "…me?"

Elyse's heart did the very thing she'd feared. It snapped in a few more places.

She leaned over and kissed her cheek. "No, I'm not cross. I love you." She hoped the woman would understand those simple words, because she did. She loved Priscilla, Carlos, Isabella and Sarita and most of all, Luca. She'd fallen in love with his whole family while getting to know them this week. But she couldn't stay here any longer.

The smile came back even as Elyse's tears floated closer to the surface. She was going to leave. She had to. The thought of telling Luca the truth was suddenly the last thing she wanted to do. He deserved to have those babies. Italian babies. Babies that were part of a large and happy family. She'd seen evidence of that wider family last night. They loved each other, had laughed and conversed. Even if he loved her, she didn't want to keep him from what someone else could give him.

He would get over her. He had once before. Quite easily, in fact.

She knew exactly what she was going to do. She was going to make sure Priscilla had some quality time with Annalisa today, and then her aunt was suddenly going to call her and ask her to return to the States. Her ticket back home wasn't for a couple more weeks, but surely she could find a flight out of Italy sooner?

And then she was going to try to forget this trip had ever happened. She would make sure Luca and his family were able to see Annalisa, but as far as rekindling a dead romance, she was going to let those smoldering ashes grow cold, once and for all.

CHAPTER THIRTEEN

SHE MADE IT to the airport.

God, she couldn't believe she'd gotten out of the house without Luca cornering her. Sporting dark glasses to keep anyone from seeing the state of her eyes, she went to the desk to ask about getting on the first flight she could find. Anywhere in the United States would work. She could worry about getting back to Atlanta once she was there.

She should have told him about the hysterectomy from the very beginning, but her stupid pride had kept telling her it was none of his business.

Well, she'd made it his business when she'd had sex with him. But to try to clear it up now?

No way. He'd said he wanted more children. He might be able to unsay it, but he couldn't un-want it.

"I need a flight to the United States. The first one you have available, please." Peg, who'd never intended on staying for the entire month, had flown home almost three weeks ago, and Elyse missed her desperately right now. Anna was in her baby sling and Elyse had one suitcase with her. She'd left everything else behind. Not that he'd try to come after her.

Except he might. She had his daughter. This wasn't like last time, when he had been the one who'd left.

The woman behind the desk leaned closer. "Are you okay? Do you need help?"

Yes. She needed a ticket. Then she realized the agent thought she was in some kind of trouble.

Of course, you dummy. You didn't give her a destination other than the whole country.

She was eventually going to have to get back in touch with Luca and work out arrangements for visitation. But she could do that with a long-distance phone call—the longer the distance the better.

"I'm fine, sorry." She reached in the front pocket of the diaper bag and pulled out her original ticket and handed it to the woman. "I need to get home sooner than I expected, that's all. Are there any flights to somewhere in Georgia or, if not, one of the neighboring states?"

The ticket agent looked relieved. "Let me see what I can do." She did some clicking of keys, her mouth twisting one way and then another as she seemed to mentally shoot down each option. "Wait. I think I can get you to Atlanta, actually. The flight leaves in two hours. You'll have a few hours' layover in Miami, if that's okay."

"Yes, that's perfect. Thank you so much."

She tried to smile but was well aware that it didn't quite come out the way she'd hoped.

"How much for the ticket?"

The price was steep. Very steep. But it was worth it.

"I'll take it."

She took out her wallet, only to have a voice behind her say in English, "The lady isn't going anywhere."

Elyse froze. No. It couldn't be.

She whirled around.

Luca! How had he…?

How had he gotten here so fast? Unless he'd left Rome at around the same time she had.

She could hear the ticket agent asking her again if she was okay. She wasn't. Not at all. But unless she wanted the authorities called and Luca hauled away for something he didn't do, she needed to allay the woman's fears. She took a deep breath and faced her once again. This time there was a phone in the agent's hand. "Would you like me to call someone?"

"No, I'm sorry. He's the baby's father." Then realizing that sounded off as well, she explained. "We're both her parents. Everything is okay."

She got out of line, hoping that she hadn't just sunk their chances of talking this through without getting arrested.

Walking a few feet away, she half hoped he wouldn't follow her. But of course he did.

He stared down at her, then his hand went to his baby's dark head, sifting through the wispy strands. Anna looked up at him, her face breaking into a toothless grin.

Guilt clawed at the edges of her heart. This was wrong. She shouldn't have left without talking to him first, should have realized he would figure out where she was.

This time when the tears came she didn't try to stop them. "You shouldn't have come."

"Yes. I should have. I'm prepared to go back to the States with you if necessary until you tell me why we can't be together." He removed her sunglasses and lifted her chin. "Don't shut me out, Ellie. You did it in Atlanta too, and it tore me apart. Talk to me. Is it something I did or said?"

"No, you didn't do anything. I—It's…" She swallowed hard. "Why are you here, Luca?"

"Isn't it obvious? I love you."

Oh, God, she was right. But it was too late. She shook her head, the tears coming faster. "It's not going to be enough."

"Why? If you're talking about the layoff, it doesn't matter anymore. We'll work at different hospitals." He used his thumbs to brush away her tears.

"It…" She closed her eyes and tried again. "You want more children, and I can't have them."

He frowned. "What?"

This was where he would hear what she had to say and walk away.

Or would he?

There was only one way to find out.

"The reason I didn't come to Italy with Anna before now was that when she was born there were complications. I had to have a hysterectomy. I can't carry any more children." Ever.

"But the condom... *Dio*. You said we didn't *need* it, not that you didn't want me to use one."

"You misunderstood. And I misunderstood when you said you wanted more. I thought you were talking about more... *sex*. But you actually meant you wanted more children."

She sucked down a breath. "And then your mom told me to have more of your babies and—"

"One minute." He appeared to be working through something. "First of all—how do you say it? My *madre* isn't the boss of me. Not since I turned eighteen."

"I know, but—"

"I am not finished." He pressed his forehead to hers. "I did say I wanted more children, but it was in response to what I thought you wanted when we were in bed. Would I like more children? Yes, maybe in the future. But there are other ways of expanding our family and plenty of time to work it out. For now, you and Anna are enough. You will *always* be enough."

It couldn't be this easy. Could it?

"It's not fair to you."

"No." He plucked her old ticket from her hand. "This is what isn't fair. You leaving without telling me."

"You did it to me once."

His eyes closed. "And I was wrong. What I felt when I realized you were gone... *Dio.* I put you through hell, didn't I?"

"I think we put each other through hell."

"No more. The only question I have is this. Do you love me?"

She licked her lips. One last hurdle. *Do it, Elyse.*

"Yes, I love you. But what about your job? My job?"

"Those are things we can work out. Together." He slid his arm behind her nape and pulled her cheek to his. "When I realized you weren't in your room and that most of your belongings were gone, I couldn't believe it. My hands shook, and my gut twisted inside me.

"I made a mistake by leaving Atlanta last year. I told myself a hundred times I should go back and talk things out with you, but my pride wouldn't let me. And the longer it went on, the less likely it seemed that you would want me back. But this time—this time—I wasn't going to repeat that mistake. I am ready to move heaven and earth to make this work." He took a deep breath. "I just needed that 'yes' to my question about you loving me."

He kissed her forehead and then his daughter's. "Whether we're here or in the States, the only thing that matters is that we're together. Our little family."

"I want that too."

His finger traced down the side of her face. "Anna is going to need both of us. And when the time comes, we'll add more."

Before she could react, he smiled. "I've always wanted to help children who are in difficult situations. What do you think?"

"Adopt?" She said the word softly, not quite

believing that he was saying the very thing she had thought of doing.

"Yes. Would you like that?"

She closed her eyes and sucked down a deep breath, believing at last. "Yes. I would love that."

"So…there's only one more question. Will you marry me? My *mamma*, she's old-fashioned, remember? And she's very good at throwing big parties. Or a big wedding."

Somehow she didn't think this had anything to do with his mom's prowess as a hostess.

"Well, we wouldn't want to disappoint your mom, would we?"

"So your answer is yes?"

"It's definitely yes."

With that, his lips came down on hers with a promise of things to come. Of promises kept. Of futures realized.

And this time she was not going to second-guess herself. Or him. She was just going to love him. And let herself be loved.

There was nothing more important than that.

THEY'D TIED THE KNOT. Not because of Annalisa or anyone's parents, but for them. And true to form, Priscilla had put on the wedding of the century, even though they would have been just as happy standing before a justice of the peace. Elyse had talked Luca into letting his mom have her way. It made her happy. And Luca had chosen Enzo as his best man, despite those earlier fears. It gave Elyse confidence that he trusted their love was strong enough to withstand any storm.

Her parents and Peggy had flown in from the States to celebrate, and Peggy had pulled her aside to whisper, "I knew it wasn't finished between you two. If Anna hadn't pulled you together again, he would have come back for you."

Luca had admitted as much in the breathless moments after the ceremony was over and they were ensconced in their swanky hotel room. "I already knew I'd messed up. My conscience wasn't going to leave me alone. It might have taken as much as another year, but I would have flown back to Atlanta and confronted you."

She'd shivered at the confirmation of her aunt's words. For her part, Elyse told him why she'd withdrawn back then as he held her tight and kissed her on the temple. "I'd had a bad office romance, and I was determined not to do it again. But then you came along, and I felt like I was making some of the same old mistakes."

"But we won't. I promise you that."

Promises were made and kept. She'd promised to talk to him instead of withdrawing emotionally, and he'd promised to call her on it if she didn't.

She'd torn her plane ticket up and called the hospital administrator and officially resigned, deciding to spend six months in Italy immersing herself in the language and culture. How could she not? Hadn't Luca done the same in America? Her Italian still wasn't the best, but she'd learned what some of those naughty words meant, and they made her blush even harder. She still had another month of language school, and then they would decide where to go from there.

Right now, none of that mattered.

Luca came up behind her on the veranda and looped his arms around her waist. "Everything okay?"

Turning to face him, she leaned back on the railing. "Just counting my blessings."

"You were up late last night and early this morning too."

"Thanks to you." She tipped her face up to look into those dark eyes she loved so much. "You know you're very sexy in the morning." She reached up to run her fingers along the stubble lining his jaw. He had on an old faded T-shirt and pajama bottoms and his tanned feet were bare. Sexy didn't begin to describe her husband.

"And you're evading my question."

She laughed. "You didn't ask a question. But I heard what you were asking. No regrets. I'm happy. Anna loves you desperately. I love you desperately. I'm just enjoying the moments we have to ourselves. Now that she's older, we don't get many of them."

So far they hadn't talked any more about expanding their little family. Adoptions in Italy had stringent requirements and they'd need to be married for three years before going through the process. And there was always surrogacy, if they decided to harvest her eggs. They had time. For once, Elyse was in no hurry to get things done.

"Emilia likes eating with her. You should give yourself a break every once in a while."

"I've had a long break. And I appreciate all her help. I just don't want to miss anything," she said.

"I know what you mean."

She wrapped her arms around his neck. "I'm so grateful for second chances."

"So am I." He leaned down and brushed his cheek against hers, before murmuring. "I love *second* chances. And maybe even third chances. Very, very much."

Since they'd made love only an hour earlier, he surely couldn't mean…

Something stirred against her. A sensation she knew all too well. "You're kidding."

"Does it feel like I'm kidding?"

The man was insatiable. And she loved it. They had a lot of time to make up for.

"Well, then, what are you waiting for?"

He swung her up in his arms. "Is that an invitation, *Dottore Venezio?*"

Dr. Venezio.

Oh, how she loved hearing him call her that. And, yes, she loved second chances. Would never tire of them.

"It is indeed, *Dottore Venezio.*"

Then he was striding back through the French doors that led to their bedroom. Their own private sanctuary, where nothing was taken for granted, and where every kiss, every touch, every sigh centered around the most powerful word of all time: love.

* * * * *

LET'S TALK

Romance

For exclusive extracts, competitions and special offers, find us online:

f facebook.com/millsandboon

⊙ @millsandboonuk

🐦 @millsandboon

Or get in touch on 0844 844 1351*

For all the latest titles coming soon, visit millsandboon.co.uk/nextmonth

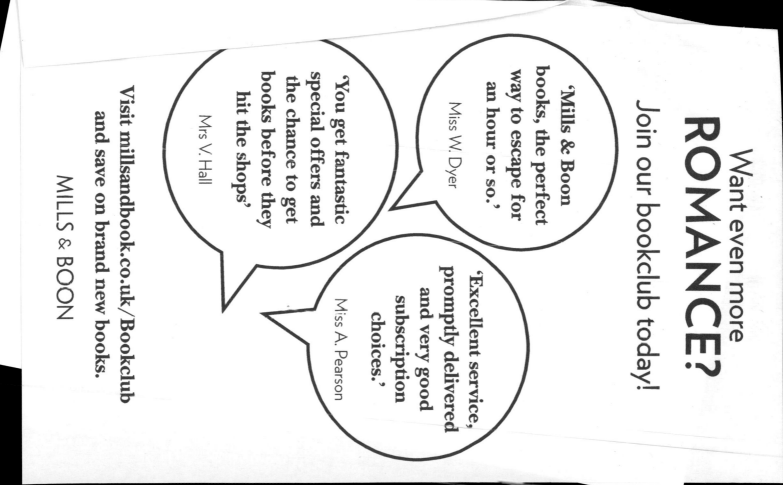